# The Cousin

# The Cousin

John Calabro

QUATTRO BOOKS

Canada Council for the Arts Conseil des Arts du Canada

*We acknowledge the support of the Canada Council for the Arts which last year invested $20.1 million in writing and publishing throughout Canada.*

Cover art: From an original by 'greatmumi'
Author's photograph: Sandra Lisi-Calabro
Cover design: Diane Mascherin
Italian/Sicilian/Petran words: Salvatore Bancheri

Library and Archives Canada Cataloguing in Publication

Calabro, John
The cousin / John Calabro.

ISBN 978-0-9810186-3-8

I. Title.

PS8605.A43C68 2009 C813'.6 C2009-904386-6

Published by Quattro Books
P.O. Box 53031, Royal Orchard Postal Station
10 Royal Orchard Blvd., Thornhill, ON L3T 3C0
www.quattrobooks.ca

Printed in Canada

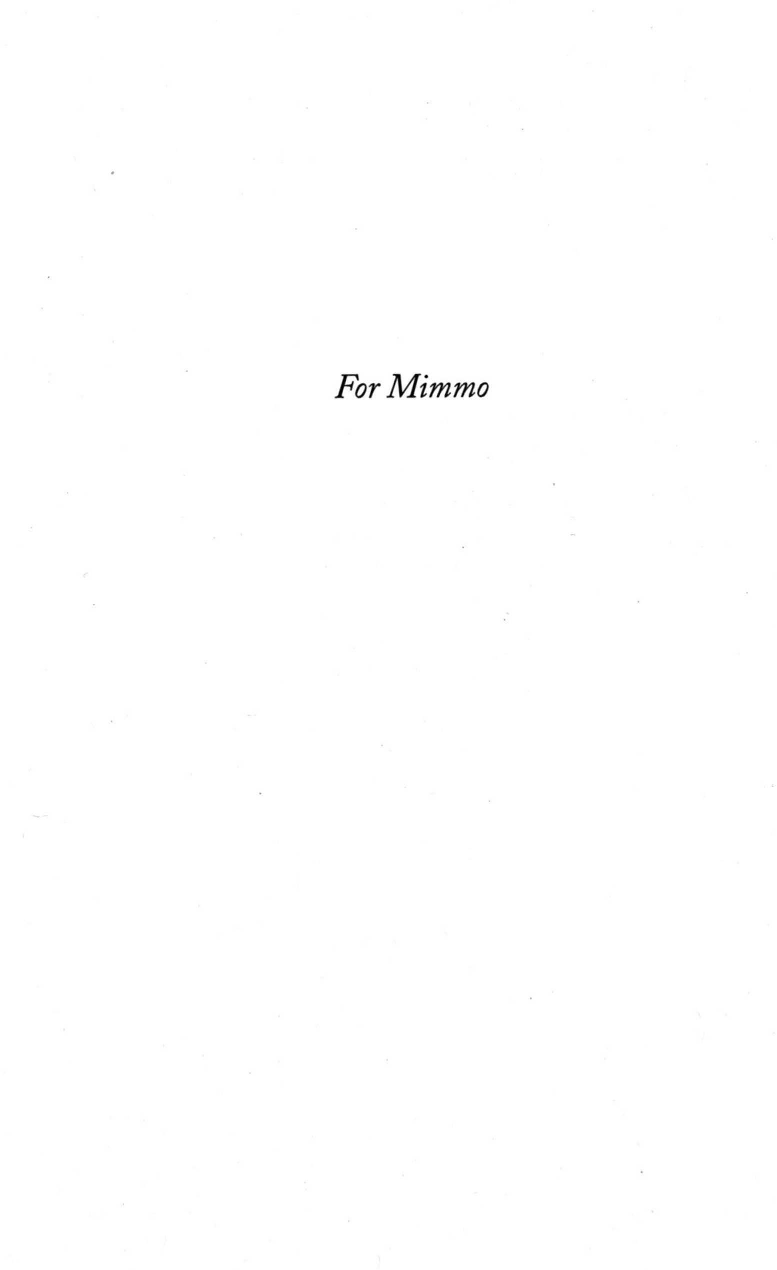

*For Mimmo*

# ONE

"WHAT?" THE SOUND of splashing water makes it difficult to hear her.

"No, I don't like it," she answers from the shower stall.

It is not so much that I hate the idea of showing up in that small feudal town, perched hundreds of feet above sea level; it is more that I don't want to see or talk to the relatives that still live in Petra. I don't particularly like people on any given day, let alone people I have not seen for over thirty years. At the best of times I am uncomfortable with making small talk, and I don't know how to start or end conversations with family, or with strangers.

"He'll be expecting us to go to him, and out of respect we should do it A-sap," she shouts.

I don't really want to see uncle. This trip had been Susan's idea more than mine, a beach holiday in Sicily where she could also discover a bit more about me, and I was already regretting it.

"I'm not looking forward to seeing *zio*. I told you, he hit me when I was a kid. He was mean."

Susan turns off the taps, pokes her head out and says, "Sal, that's how they disciplined kids in those days. It was wrong but they didn't know better. You're not still holding a grudge, are you?"

The bathroom door is ajar and Susan is combing her wet hair. I like watching her. I love observing women going through their morning rituals, as if I'm seeing a painting by Renoir come alive.

I should tell her how much I enjoy looking at her, but I keep that to myself.

She grabs the underneath part with her brush, first pulls up and then slowly drags her hair back down, letting the hot air of the small dryer straighten her long strawberry curls into a manageable mass. She is standing in front of the mirror with a small bath towel draped around her torso, a wrap she has tucked into a fold where her breasts meet. The hint of her nakedness aided by a vodka and blood-orange juice begins to arouse me.

She comes out, and methodically continues to dry herself. She ties the towel around her chest tighter as the knot threatens to undo itself.

"Sal, please open the large suitcase for me?"

I do, set it at the foot of the bed, and go back to watching her.

Susan bends down, throws a few things out, chooses a flimsy sundress, and when least expected, the knot, as if reading my mind, unties itself and lets her breasts slip outside the towel, betraying her best attempt at modesty. She quickly looks up to see my reaction and finds me smirking.

She leers back and sticks out her tongue, but, tired of adjusting the towel, allows the small wrap to stay on the floor and says, "Go ahead, stare all you want," and I do.

I stare at her breasts, medium sized half grapefruits, still firm, I look at her slightly rounded belly, still soft, at her neatly trimmed triangle of sex, still enticing, and I smile as I get harder. Her smooth white skin, home to countless freckles made more visible by the bright Sicilian sun, excites me. I love tall women. Her long Irish legs are made for dancing Slip Jigs. In the past, seeing her naked would have been enough for me to throw her on our hotel bed and kick-start our vacation by making furious love to my sexy Celtic wife, but now, playing it safe, I hesitate and try to read her mood.

I used to be well aware of the difference between a red light and a green light, even if at times I'd speed right through a red, but these days I am stuck in a world of self-imposed amber lights that I can't seem to shake.

Susan looks at me and sees the growing bulge between my legs as I lie purposefully spread-eagled on the bed; my way of asking permission.

She shakes her head, turns her back to me, and slips on a pair of lacy underwear.

She then does a quick double take, and says, "I can't believe you."

"What?"

"You're impossible. This is not the time. We were talking about calling your uncle."

Her words, the perfect cold shower to make me go limp, do their job.

I finish my drink and try again to convince her about delaying meeting my uncle and his family.

"Maybe we should take a beach day and then go see the Temples in Agrigento, ease into this vacation. I thought that's what you wanted, to see some antiquities, to get some sun...."

I say those words in a tone that doesn't betray my disappointment at another wasted erection.

She also acts as if nothing had happened.

"No, I think we should see him first, and besides, I'm anxious to meet your cousin Charlie."

"We can see him soon enough."

"Now, you're upset. Listen Sal, if you didn't want to see your relatives why did you agree to come half-way across the world and stay in a hotel, half an hour from them, and why did you say yes to this vacation, and by the way we should have brought gifts, I don't know why I let you dissuade me."

She gets exasperated at having to spell things out for me. I repeat what I had said in Toronto.

"We'll give them a card and some cash. God knows they can use the money."

"Money is not a gift, it may even embarrass them. When are you going to phone? And by the way, that taxi driver shouldn't have charged us extra for our luggage, and I don't appreciate that you didn't let me confront him."

Sensing the beginning of an argument, I pick up the phone and dial the ten-digit number. Sitting on the edge of the bed, I can see the Mediterranean Sea with its canopy of rippled light-green water closer to the beach, and its deep, smooth dark blue water farther out. I can't swim, which is in itself strange for one born in Sicily, but I am sure that the salty water would keep me afloat and gently take me all the way to Africa. In the distance, a flotilla of sailboats are bobbing up and down, and I wish I was on one of them instead of being here having to make this phone call.

Susan, now fully dressed, stands over me, as if to make sure that I dial properly. I turn to the side and away from her, mostly to annoy her.

"*Pronto*," a raspy male voice answers.

My stomach tightens, "Hi!"

The voice clears its throat, "*Pronto, chi parla*?"

Susan nudges me and whispers, "Speak in Italian."

Of course, I am not stupid, but I had forgotten.

"*Zio Calogero?*"

"*Sì.*"

"*So Salvatore, il figlio di Pasquale.*" I identify myself in a bad Sicilian accent, and Susan laughs at me. She is happy again.

"*Salvatore? Totò, sì, sì... Porco Giuda, unni*?"

No one has called me Totò since my parents passed away, and it rattles me. I explain that we have arrived in Trapani and that we are at the Hotel Montana, and how it would be great to see him, and that if it is inconvenient to let me know without any '*ceremonies*', and that I don't want to bother him, and that we could make it another time, maybe on our way back from Florence, and how is *zia*, and how the heat is stifling and how Susan is with me and says hi, and how is Charlie, and how, if it is really inopportune, we can see him on our way back, since we will be flying home to Toronto from Palermo, and that we arrived yesterday and have settled into our hotel, and how everything is really beautiful, and that we are a bit tired....

I blurt and babble on incoherently for a few more minutes until Susan taps me on the shoulder and mimes with her hands, 'What are you doing?'

I reiterate, "If it is inconvenient...."

"*Bedda matri, Nun fari lu scemuo.*" Insult number one. He calls me feeble-minded, in a nice way, but I can't help but feel that he means it, and that I deserve it.

"*Totò*, staya there. Charlie, he pick u up. No move. *Sì* Hotel Montana, I know. Okay, u come to me, Okay. U… In *Sicilia*! Yes? *Porcu cani, chi surprisa*, no move, *ciao-ciao*."

He is taking control, as I dreaded and knew he would.

"Well?" says Susan.

# TWO

SUSAN INSISTS ON taking the stairs. Another new thing with her, she wants to exercise, lose a few pounds, and stay healthy while I am happy with the opposite. Keeping fit, like many other things that are good for me, doesn't interest me. A few minutes earlier, the Front Desk had called to say that a cousin Charlie was waiting for us. We had only seen him in the photographs that his father had sent to my parents; the last one was of him as a boy in a dark suit and a white armband, outside the town's main church on his way to confirmation.

The lobby is empty except for a young man leaning against a faux Corinthian column.

"Chiaaarlie," Susan screams as she decides that it can only be him.

Charlie has grown from a teenager into a man. No longer pudgy, he's tall and thin with long, shoulder-length hair. His face, without the baby fat, has a symmetrical, suntanned attractiveness. He has the traditional aquiline nose, a trademark of the Corbo family, one that hints at a Roman or Greek lineage mixed with the blood of African conquerors. Yet his nose is smaller than mine, delicate, a perfect fit for his pretty boy handsomeness.

"*Ciau' cugi'*," he yells back in the hometown drawl, adding a wide, genuine smile to his greeting.

Susan responds with a long, tight hug that takes him by surprise.

"*Comu va Charlie*?" she asks, once she finally lets go of him, trying her version of a Sicilian dialect on him.

Her Italian is much better than mine. Susan learned it in university. It helps that she uses it every day, teaching linguistics in the Italian Department of the University of Toronto.

He comes forward, and I am ready to offer my hand, but change my mind in mid-stream and, following Susan's lead, I grab his hand, say, "Come here, you," and pull him towards me for a manly hug.

There is a slight, awkward, men-hugging-men jostle, and then he leans over and kisses me on both cheeks, an Italian ritual I knew well, but out of habit had almost forgotten.

"I have a dear friend's car outside," he says in formal Italian, dropping the Sicilian dialect, perhaps to better impress Susan.

He is wearing tight blue jeans and a white shirt exposing a tanned but noticeably hairless chest. His light-brown, straight hair is unlike the rest of the Corbo clan's dark curls that could have come either from Rome or from Carthage.

Charlie grabs Susan's overnight bag, since we were told earlier that we would be spending the night at my uncle's, something which, unlike Susan, I wasn't keen on, and leads us to a small red Fiat. He has an odd, sauntering walk.

I whisper in Susan's ear, "Do you think he straightens his hair?"

She whispers back for me to shut up.

I sit myself in the front, bang my knees against the glove compartment of a sardine-can of a car, another Italian trademark I had forgotten.

I don't really know this grown-up cousin Charlie, who, now in his mid-twenties, is mostly a stranger, except that he is still family and my only cousin. We haven't kept up through the years. A postcard now and then, a phone call at Christmas and one at Easter was the cxtent of it.

"You have a good voyage, yes?" he asks in English.

"*Sì, tu comu si.*" I answer in a dreadful dialect and apologize for not making a greater effort at retaining my Italian or at least my Sicilian.

He tells us that he learned English in school but never quite got the hang of that difficult language, and didn't get much of the other school stuff either and quit before graduating, but that was okay, he says, and smiles.

That type of admission, said so casually, doesn't sit right with me, and so far I'm not sure I like this cousin of mine.

We drive through downtown Trapani, where the Stazione Marittima and Piazza Garibaldi overlook the Mediterranean.

"Look, a camel."

Near the entrance to the Siculian Regional Botanical Garden, a man dressed in traditional Arab robes is leading a short-legged, one-hump camel in circles, offering tourists a short ride on his misplaced desert Taxi. Adding to the surreal scene is a canvas backdrop with a mural depicting Saharan sand dunes and a bright red circle for a sun, while closer to the sidewalk one real but scrawny palm tree stands tall, encased in a cement planter. Fake road signs that point towards Tunis, Sousse, and Algeria are conveniently placed to complete the make-believe set. Tourists can have their pictures taken riding a camel while pretending to be in Africa for only ten Euros. It is all quite ridiculous, but unexpectedly appealing.

"I'm so doing that later," I say. And although Susan shares my surprise at this unique tourist attraction, she says she wants no part of a camel ride.

Charlie turns to look.

"I see that camel all the time when I come to the city, and I think that I would also like to take a ride, but then I never do. I must admit, cousins, that I am a bit scared," he says in Sicilian.

"Why would you guys want to do that? It looks so fake, so unreal," Susan answers in Italian.

"Cousins, if I had the courage, I would love to get on that strange animal and ride it all the way to Africa, but I am too afraid," continues Charlie.

I could remind him that the Mediterranean Sea is in the way of this imaginary voyage of his, but I choose not to. How can I explain to them that it is the absurdity that attracts me to it and not the actual ride?

More importantly, as I look beyond the camel, there is a memory of the Siculian Regional Botanical Garden that surfaces; it is where I first saw blood-oranges hanging down from small trees. I don't know why we were there but I remember my mother saying that Sicilians were very much like those red-tainted oranges, both sweet and bitter. I didn't understand what she meant, but she picked one, and gave it to me, along with a kiss on the cheek.

We drive out of the city and begin the climb of Monte San Calogero, originally named Mount Ercole, in honour of Hercules.

"So beautiful…"

Susan points to the tiny flowers at the ends of the prickly pears on cactus leaves the size of beaver tails, and at the carpet of wild flowers in bloom on the side of the road, and at the rustic stone walls that delineate different orchards, and at the tall wild grass, and at the small fruit trees that dot the roadside, and at the greenness of the rolling hills ahead of us, and at the blueness of the sea behind us. She emotes like a little schoolgirl. Even the abandoned and crumbling farmhouses she finds quaint.

"I hadn't imagined *your* Sicily this way," she says, meaning she was seeing colours where I had painted a picture of bleak harshness and that she had wrongly believed my interpretation. I had to admit that it was a surprise to me too. I hadn't realized how much my parents' dark view of Sicily had influenced my memories, and how much I had made them my own. Today, everything is brighter.

"Charlie, you must love it here, so much beauty, so much history…"

Charlie takes his time answering. He comments again on how well she speaks Italian, and that she is so right, Sicily is beautiful, even better in the spring, and that the various panoramas are truly marvellous, but that Sicily would be a lot more beautiful if it wasn't for the Sicilians who live in it. He says that they are, for the most part, a small people, intolerant, suspicious and immoveable and that the Mafia encourages that attitude in order to control them. The gangsters get rich on the ignorance of Sicilians.

Susan is surprised by his harsh opinion, but I nod in agreement.

"Is it always this hot?" Susan asks in a deliberate attempt to lighten the mood.

"No, it's not, but I remember two years ago it was over forty almost every day of the summer and it didn't rain for five months. I didn't mind; I like the burning heat, I am strange that way. Living in Africa would not *unaccommodate* me at all."

I don't know what to make of him; my estimation of Charlie keeps changing, from liking to not liking and back.

"Speaking of Africa, I'd love to go there myself, I almost went to Morocco after my parents passed away," I say.

Charlie turns to me and wants to hear more. He says that most Sicilians are prejudiced against Arabs, but for him, everyone is the same, skin colour is not important.

Susan looks at me as if saying not that story again, but I don't care, I continue.

"It was my dream to take the train to Marrakech from Tangiers, see the Sahara desert, touch the sand dunes, ride a camel, cross over to Algeria and slowly make my way to Carthage, to Tunis. And then take the boat to Trapani. It would have been a great trip."

"Tunis," Charlie perks up. "Tell me what happened?"

"I'd just met Susan and we had been dating for a while. Before taking the ferry to Tangiers, I called her in Toronto, and she sounded so sad, all confused. She said she missed me, and that she loved me, and wasn't sure where we were headed as a couple. I cut my trip short and went back to Canada. Six months later we were engaged, a year later we were married."

"That's so romantic," moans Charlie.

Susan had heard my story innumerable times and makes a face. Ignoring Charlie's sickeningly sweet comment, she adds very quickly, "You see Charlie, he still blames me for not fulfilling *his* dream," and laughs, "*his* dream of riding a camel in Africa."

She tries to pass it off as a joke but I know that it is a sore spot with her.

"No, I don't blame you."

"Yes you do, admit it."

What I admit is that I do wonder from time to time what my life would have been like if I had gone to Africa. Would Susan and I be sitting in this car?

Charlie doesn't want to see us fight, and says, "Like I was saying, I also want to go to Africa, I have a friend who lives in Tunis and he's always asking me to join him there. But how can I?"

"Why?"

"My parents."

"Charlie, how *are* you parents?"

My aunt had Charlie when she was quite old, and now they were two old people with a young son.

"They're getting on. My father, he's fine for an old mule of seventy-five. He's mad at me right now. Well he's always angry with me."

"What did you do?" asks Susan.

"The usual. I stay out too late, I sleep in too much, I spend too much money, and I don't work too much. That's what he thinks."

"I am sure you'll find work. What kind of work do you like to do?" Susan asks, not so much to be inquisitive but because she, unlike me, genuinely cares about people and their lives.

Charlie talks with his hands even as he is rounding the dangerous curves of Mount Ercole, and I worry about our safety.

"How can I even think of a job, a career? Taking care of my parents is full-time work. This is Sicily. You have to know someone to get a job."

"I am sorry."

"No. No, and even if I could work, who is going to hire me? We have 'dead of hunger' immigrants who are exploited and work for nothing; first it was the Albanians, and now the Romanians. And then, you must have heard about the Algerians and the people from Angola that we pick up from the sea and drop off at Lampedusa. The welcoming station there is filled to the brim. I don't blame these poor people, they're desperate, but what can I do? There is no work for me."

I could mention that his lack of education might have something to do with the fact that he can't find a job, and that those immigrants are taking jobs that Sicilians don't particularly want. We do listen to the news in Canada, but this is not the place for that discussion, and I let it go.

He continues plaintively, "I mean if I went north, in Torino, Milano, there might be something, but not here, not in Sicily, here we have nothing, that bastard fascist, Berlusconi, keeps the tax money north of Rome, and what comes down ends up in the hands of the Mafia. I curse them all to hell, politicians and brigands."

At least I like his politics. Susan also agrees with him. Charlie momentarily lets go of the steering wheel, puts the palms of his hands together as if praying, and shakes them up and down, a Sicilian sign that means, "What can I do? I am resigned to my lot." He nonchalantly grabs back the steering wheel before the car veers over the edge and off the cliff. This may not be the way I want to die.

Petra, originally named Petras by the Greeks, as Charlie proudly explains, is cloistered above Monte San Calogero. We wind our way up from the south side, a trickier but shorter route. A road that cuts through ancient agricultural lands still cultivated by Petrans, and with few exceptions in the same fashion as their forefathers.

Susan indulges Charlie, "I understand," she says, nodding her head.

I think he uses his aging parents as an excuse. No one works in Sicily, and those that do act as if they don't. Our Sicilian taxi driver said that, and I agree with him. Everyone complains about everyone else but they all seem to be part of the problem, including the driver who ripped us off.

Charlie tries to convince us that it's not his fault. "It's like I'm a trapped animal here, I have a yoke around my neck, at least until... God forbid," he makes the sign of the cross, "Not that I am wishing it."

He has taken the role of the martyr, another characteristic I dislike about Petrans. My mother, although not Sicilian, was like that too. Southerners are all martyrs, or at least they pretend to be. Everything is about self-sacrifice, something they never tire of reminding us of, so that we may feel guilty for being born. Susan is taking it all in; she doesn't know how Pirandelian Sicilians can be, and Charlie is no different.

I decide to let Susan do the talking while I look at the countryside. I don't remember so many olive trees, they are smaller than I imagined with their tiny light-green leaves. The trunks and the branches are twisted and intertwined; it is as if I'm seeing them for the first time, beautiful trunks, like embracing bodies.

"Look at those olive trees, Susan."

"That one is so twisted it looks like Medusa. We should have really visited Sicily a lot sooner. Sal, I don't understand why you never wanted to come back."

I ignore her comment, sit back to hear a ping-pong of questions and answers between her and Charlie, some of which trigger the odd memory. The novelty of remembering fades and all I hear are words.

"Some can grow to be three hundred years old."

"Incredible, and what are those?"

"Almonds, carobs."

"And those?"

"Fig trees."

I get tired of the wide-eyed tourist banter, and turn to my right where a small dirt path dangerously winds its way around the mountain before a steep drop to the sea. I can see the road below us and there, a boy, about ten, is running towards the city of Trapani, towards where we have come from. He runs, stops, walks, looks behind him and runs again. Every time I think he's about to fall he regains his balance and continues his descent towards the city. I look behind him for an adult, a mother or a father but there is no one. I lose sight of him as we round a corner and then he comes back into view. This time, following him, there is a man pulling a mule and quickening his steps. The boy stops, looks behind him, and as the older man gets closer, he takes off again. They both look up the hill, and as I see their faces, I recognize them…

"The boy… The man… It's me and uncle…."

"What?"

"Who?"

No sooner do I say those words than I realize I have spoken out loud and sound like an idiot. Susan moves over to her right and looks down, but of course there is no one. I don't see them either.

"Nothing… I thought I saw something."

Each turn and each bend brings new sights, new questions from Susan, and new answers from Charlie. They forget about me. They have an easy and comfortable way of talking to each other that I almost envy.

"It must be difficult looking after aging parents, and you're so young," she says.

"It's not bad. It's just that I have to be around all the time. I drive them to the doctor; to do their banking, I pay the bills, do the shopping, you know, whatever they need. You know my father, everything has to be done his way, even if it is the wrong way."

Uncle was known for his quick temper, for his emotional outbursts. Unlike me, who, according to Susan, for a Sicilian, showed very little emotion. In her opinion, I could stand to be a bit more expressive, even more demonstrative, and maybe shouldn't try to hide my feelings all the time. She has said that if she left me, it would be because I was so unresponsive to her, and to life in general. Once she even said that she could almost take my having an affair, but shutting her out like I did emotionally was probably worse than infidelity.

I swore to her that I didn't do it on purpose, which was true, and that I would try harder, which I never did, and wondered instead if she meant I could have an affair. In reality, I had resigned myself to the fact that I was incapable of what she was asking me. My parents were like that, and how could I be any different.

Charlie continues, "He's not a bad man, he yells a lot, bangs on the table, makes sarcastic comments, you know, a normal Sicilian father."

My father was not 'normal' like that; he was the opposite of his brother, quiet and unduly stoic, maybe too stoic.

"When I was young, I used to get the belt, but I deserved it. Now, he just uses words. I don't care. He can't hurt me."

Charlie is wrong; his father's insults are still reverberating in my ears.

My parents never talked much about Charlie or my uncle and aunt. But then my mother and father didn't say very much about anything while we lived in Canada. There was an oppressive silence in our household that I didn't understand. My parents communicated on a need-to-know basis, without much warmth. It was only after I married Susan that I realized how much of their destructive behaviour had been passed on to me, and yet I was unable to shake it. Knowing was not enough.

"Do you travel much these days?" Susan asks.

"No, I don't go far. Trapani, the clubs, the beach, sometimes Palermo, to see a soccer game. Once to Etna, I loved the volcano. I got full of black soot."

He gets all excited but it doesn't last.

"I can't stay away too long, in case they need me. This is my cross to carry."

We ride in silence. The radio blares Italian pop songs and Charlie bobs his head to the music, a Saint Christopher medallion around his neck swings to the rhythm.

Suddenly, he says, "Do you want to hear something different?"

And before we can answer he puts on a CD with an unusual mix of Middle Eastern sounds, African Jazz and modern Hip-hop beats. When Susan queries him, he says that the singer is Tunisian. He tells us that his name is Farouk Brahmen, and that he likes his type of music very much.

I find his taste in music quite incongruous. In contrast to the idiotic pop music he had on the radio earlier, this Farouk is quite good, very edgy.

Susan looks out of her side window and I look ahead, testing my memory, drawing mostly blanks.

The entrance to Petra is a curving narrow road with a phalanx of pine trees whose trunks are painted in a white spray to keep diseases away. Charlie explains that this Petra started as a Phoenician colony down below. Susan leans forward, and I pretend to be bored by a story that I should have known better.

He proudly continues, mostly for Susan's sake.

"The Arabs then rebuilt it, higher up on its present plateau...."

I nod as if *that* was common knowledge, but must admit that I didn't know the Arabs had anything to do with Petra.

Isolated, enclosed by walls dating to Byzantine times, the new Petra is well sheltered from unwanted outsiders. Most of Sicily is like that, in a defensive mode, ready to fend off intruders, and deeply closed onto itself. Susan often accuses me of being like that. An irony, considering how much I disliked the town I was born in.

"Look, the castle."

Charlie points to the outline of a crumbling medieval castle, Castello San Michele, which towers above the town.

The Castello triggers more memories.

I didn't always hate this town.

As a boy I discovered this Norman castle, and turned it into my personal fiefdom. The castle is as I remembered it. The indestructible white rock used as a base and as an entrance was still intact. Some of the man-made structure, weakened by storms and violence, had crumbled. To the left of the ruins, once accessible from the castle by a drawbridge, is the Tori di Ercole, a tower whose upper turret I had found a way to reach. As a child, and from up there, I could see Trapani down below, the Mediterranean straight ahead, and some days I could see what I thought was Africa. I was happy there.

Charlie says, "The town fixed the lower part. They put up lights, and at the end of August they have mediaeval games...."

The grey cobbled streets, the stone houses, and the yellow and red tiled roofs made of coarse clay become brighter as they come into sight. We cross Porta Trapani, a thick, heavy gate decorated with Carthaginian symbols.

"Is the castle still crawling with lizards?"

"*Sì.*"

The castle and its turret provided added protection for the townspeople of Petra. A good marksman could take down a whole battalion of invaders one by one before they got near the town. The island of Sicily had been conquered and governed by many, but small towns like Petra had always stayed independent. These towns closed their gates and thumbed their noses at change, wearing their insularity as a badge of honour, protecting while stifling their people.

We leave one of the three main roads that divide the town and take a side street. We can barely drive through; our rear view mirrors are inches away from scraping the houses; Charlie honks to warn others as he approaches tiny intersections that jump at us out of nowhere. The old houses are leaning towards each other; warped clay roofs are butting heads, as if in need to gossip, in need to share a joke, and as such, they give the town a claustrophobia that I didn't remember.

Charlie, in true Sicilian fashion, waves his hands and arms as he talks, and Susan notices something.

"Is that a tattoo?"

"Yes... Do you want to see it?"

He proudly shows us his tattoo where a small scissors followed by a series of thick dashes crosses the inside of his left wrist, like something one would find above discount coupons in newspapers.

He sheepishly smiles.

Susan says, "Oh... Charlie."

Wit and irony is not something I would have associated with this Charlie, and it makes *me* smile.

# THREE

*ZIO* CALOGERO AND his wife are waiting for us, standing in front of their house, looking similar to the couple in Grant Wood's painting, *American Gothic*, except that a cane replaces the pitchfork and this canvas might be called *Sicilian Gothic*.

My aunt is gushing; welcoming Susan over and over, repeating the word, "*Piacere*."

"*La bellezza*," uncle says, as he looks me up and down.

I am not sure what he means by that odd greeting. The words translate into *the beauty*, but convey so much more. They are two words but a full sentence of hidden meanings. Said in a certain tone of voice, the words can be full of sarcasm and disdain. They can also be uttered in a tone of reverence. The key, and an art mastered by many Sicilians, is to say it as if meaning respect but implying something less. In my case the expression may mean, "Thank you for coming," and may also stand for, "I am surprised that you came," or, "I am glad you came," but probably means, "You are a 'beautiful' man for coming, but you would have been an 'ugly' person if you had not shown up when I asked you to."

Susan misses the nuances of uncle's words and I just smile, pretending that it is a compliment.

Using his cane for emphasis, he brusquely turns to Charlie, gently whacks him on the thigh, and orders him to quickly return the car, "Because we don't take advantage of a favour...."

"Papa, do you have a few Euros for the petrol?" Charlie asks.

"*Sta minchia,*" *zio* Calogero answers crudely, and turns to me for support. "Look at this little puppy, he thinks I was born yesterday," and then returns to insulting his son, "*Strunzu*, what about the money I gave you yesterday, you think I forgot?"

He taps his cane impatiently.

"Gone," Charlie says, ignoring the fact that he has been called a *turd* by his father.

Zio turns to me, points to his son, "*Capiddi longhi et ciriveddu curtu.*"

It takes me a moment to understand the words but soon I make the connection and recognize the proverb, 'long of hair and short of brains'.

I smile since that is what I'm expected to do.

The unpleasant exchange between them is not unlike those uncle used to have with me as I was growing up in his house.

His face is the same one I remember, but he looks much older with sunk-in cheeks, pointy chin and a thin moustache, a vain addition, which he keeps fingering.

I expected him taller, more of a presence, more foreboding, more like a rusty spike. Instead I find him scraggy and gaunt, a bent nail at most, not someone to be afraid of.

*Zia* has a leathered, wrinkled round face, and a pasted, benign smile. It is interesting that, except for that smile, I don't remember much about *zia*. Her long, white hair is uncontrollable and despite her best efforts her tresses keep escaping the elastic that loosely holds them together.

"You must be starved." *Zia* says in the dialect of my father's family, her warmth softening the harshness of the language. I realize how much more Arabic than Italian the Petran dialect sounds. It also feels strange to hear Sicilian as a daily language and not as an exotic memory.

"We are," Susan answers a bit too quickly, speaking for the both of us.

Susan doesn't know that, no matter the occasion, a good Sicilian has to wait to be asked at least three times, and say no each time before saying yes. There must be a *reluctance* before an *acceptance*, it's part of a game, of a code that strangers do not understand.

Charlie comes back and his father immediately goes on the attack.

"What took you so long? Lost your way?" Uncle asks his son in a tone of voice markedly different than the one he uses with Susan and me.

Charlie says to his father, "When? Now?"

"No, ignorant, before."

"*Cera un saccu di traffico*."

His father is not happy at the answer and remarks that by his calculations we should have arrived 30 minutes ago, and that good food is meant to be eaten piping hot and on time.

"There must have been an accident, traffic was not moving." Charlie adds, fabricating an excuse. I knew the scenario too well, mealtime was always prime arguing time, and instinctively my stomach muscles tighten up.

He makes up a lie to cover reality, where reality needed no covering. Being made to feel guilty for things one has not done is something that I remember quite well, and although it did not stop me from misbehaving, it made me feel guiltier.

"It's all my fault, I made everyone late, you know how we women are, we want to look pretty, and sometimes we forget the time," chimes in Susan, adding to the lies in defence of Charlie.

This was pure Pirandellian, the masking of reality, lying to tell the truth. Unwittingly, Susan has picked up her own Sicilian mask.

It works. Susan's sweet voice disarms uncle.

"I usually eat at twelve on the dot, and he knows it. But, you are all here, safe and sound, and that's what counts. I am happy you are here. We are reunited, that's what's important... Sit, sit."

He smiles at us.

Charlie looks surprised at his father's quick stand-down, but then Susan and I are both strangers as well as family. There is a front to put up, which all Sicilians know, called *fare una bella figura,* to make a good appearance.

"So Totò, Totò *pazzo?*"

"*Sì,*" I say weakly, not wanting to be reminded.

How can I forget his nickname for me? Totò is an endearing diminutive for Salvatore, but he managed to make it less endearing by nicknaming me *Totò crazy*, a sarcastic assonance, his idea of a joke, which I hated, and hadn't heard since I left Sicily.

Susan thinks it's harmless and funny, and laughs with him, repeating the words *Totò pazzo.*

I look around, reorienting my memories of this place with the present. The house is quite small. There is an upstairs loft with a low ceiling where my mother and I slept, but which is now used for storage. The ground floor where they've always lived has two rooms and an attached garage that used to be a stable and housed Rosetta the mule. One bedroom, in the back, is for *zio* and *zia*, while the living room where we are eating now doubles as Charlie's bedroom. The kitchen is set up in a corner of the garage, alongside an old, small tractor that hasn't been used for years but that no one wants and that *zio,* as he explains, hopes to one day restore and sell.

At the table uncle playfully smacks me on the back of the head and says, "*Allora strunzu*, you are back, and with such a good-looking wife, who would have figured?" He laughs.

I smile, nod and ask about his health, ignoring the fact that he, albeit endearingly, has called me, as he had called his son earlier, a piece of shit. Insults as compliments are a Sicilian specialty.

He smacks me again, enjoying it more than me, and says, "I am fine but I don't have to tell you that we have gone through a difficult time."

Susan and I say that we are sorry to hear that.

"And him, *ddu babbu*," he points to the apparently *feeble minded* Charlie," he doesn't help. He doesn't work. When I was his age, I was already married and working day and night. Three jobs I had; worked like a mule. Sometimes I was the mule…" He laughs. "Hitched to a plough that my father pushed behind me, while I pulled with all my strength. I was strong like Hercules then. He cracked the whip, my father."

He demonstrates with great dramatic effects how he would pull the plough.

"Me, I'm too kind. And Charlie, he sleeps, he drinks, and eats, he thinks that bread falls from the clouds. And his *cazzu di tattoo*, did you see what he did to his wrist, what dishonour, he's crazy, no? "

I steer the conversation away from Charlie and ask him about his almond trees, I remember large fields of them.

"We don't have any property anymore, except for this house. We had to sell all the lands, bit by bit. Life is tough here. There is not much money. The small pension doesn't go far, but as my father used to say, better nothing than to lick sardines. We survive thanks to the Lord."

Charlie doesn't say much and eats silently.

"Charlie, get more bread," his father barks, then sees Susan's jumpy reaction and adds, "Please."

*Zio* grabs the large round loaf from his son, places it against his chest, and takes out his knife, a long curved stiletto, as he explains that it is the only tool and weapon that a Sicilian ever needs. He plunges the knife into the dense bread, and slices towards his chest, cutting thick chunks, while Susan and I stare.

He catches us looking and says proudly, "This knife was given to me by my father, and before that his uncle, you know the one that raised him, he gave it to him. Look, sharp like me. Feel! This knife could tell you some stories."

He also uses the knife to cut through the hard Crotone cheese and he is right, the blade slices through it as if it was soft butter. Forgoing the use of a fork, he spears the portions with his weapon and offers us a morsel of his favourite cheese.

Grandpa Salvatore, for whom I was named and the previous owner of the knife, was an orphan raised by a childless aunt. How he became an orphan no one knew or wanted to tell. There were tales and hints of a vendetta. This house we were sitting in, according to *zio*, was built of stones taken one by one out of the small arid and rocky field that *Nonno* Salvatore had managed to purchase with what was rumoured to be tainted money. People said that as a young man and in exchange for doing the local Don a favour that coincided with Grandpa's own desire for revenge, he was given enough money to cover the cost of buying that small piece of land. Rumours also had it that he might have killed a man or two to get such a generous reward.

I can't help but wonder if *nonno* used this very knife to slice his enemies as easily as *zio* sliced the bread. People feared my grandfather, and by association they also feared my uncle. And he in turn made us fear him. My father was the odd man out.

Susan speaks to *zia* in Italian.

"Susan, you are a true princess, so beautiful, and your Italian is so refined. Where did Salvatore find you?"

She blushes and he turns to me.

"But *you*, you were a bit strange as a child, and wild like a weed. A real little savage, full of fight, and now? Are you civilized? Did your wife tame the great lizard hunter?"

"Maybe a bit too civilized. He's a banker now," Susan looks at him and smiles as if joking, when I know she isn't. "Tell me about how strange he was, *zio*. I have never seen this wild side of his."

Charlie gets up and helps his mother bring the serving dishes from the kitchen to the table. Soon the delicious aroma of home cooking overwhelms the small dining room.

*Zia* offers us *pasta con verdura e sarde,* and apologises for the simplicity of the dish.

"No *zia*, this is delicious."

Susan is not fond of sardines, one of the ingredients in this dish, but I notice that she can also lie with the best of them in order to keep appearances.

"You're too kind, *bella*."

"She is, isn't she." *Zio* is quick to concur.

They both love Susan's happy and warm disposition. She is more like them than I am.

*Zio* says that he has a good tale about me, and do we know the story about when I was born.

I groan and ask him to change the subject. I dislike being talked about as much as I dislike talking about myself or about my past.

Susan implores him to tell it. She wants to know more about me and this is probably the only way she is going to find out.

He pours another round of red wine. Susan is drinking more than normal and her cheeks are turning red. Charlie stares at his untouched glass of wine.

"This is about when Salvatore was born. My brother was in Tripoli, we wrote him to come, but he was late, the midwife was stuck in Trapani for reasons I don't remember, and I, not afraid to get dirty, took over."

*Zio* empties his glass of red wine and we wait while he refills it.

"It was my responsibility and I had agreed to pay the midwife a kilo of shelled almonds for her work. It was a fair price, but the baby was coming out."

He waits for the dish of fresh codfish and black olives in a piping hot tomato sauce to be brought in by *zia* and Charlie. Uncle wants complete attention before resuming. Momentarily the conversation turns away from him and to the various methods of preparing *Baccalà*.

Impatiently, uncle asks if we want to hear the story because if we don't he will just be quiet.

"Please continue," says Susan.

"Let me see, where was I, yes there was me, my wife, your mother, that's all. She was in that room there," he points behind him with the knife, "our bedroom."

Uncle waves the blade around as he speaks.

"*Calò*, put that dangerous knife away."

He closes his knife as if closing the wings of a delicate butterfly, holding the blade in one hand and the handle in the other, pressing on the lock spring while moving the two halves towards the middle. It gives him great pleasure to be the centre of attention.

"It is a *Cuteddu di Bisacquino*." He says as if we were supposed to know the difference between brands.

He shows us the aged horn handle with lines etched into it. Susan asks to see it up close, and he opens it again for her. He warns her of its sharpness, and describes how to use it by saying that you slice towards your left and against the handle.

He says that with a capable knife and one good swipe you can slice a man in half, and don't you assume that this cutlass hasn't seen its share of blood. He ends with "Don't ever underestimate a Sicilian with a knife, he's capable of anything."

Inadvertently hearing his words, I feel a sense of Sicilian pride that shouldn't be there, that I had never had or desired.

"You want to see something? Count the seconds."

Without waiting for an answer, *zio* stands up, puts the knife back in his pants, makes sure that everyone is looking at him, and suddenly in one fluid motion that belies his age, snatches the knife from his pocket, cocks his arm, locks his wrist in place and makes a wide semi-circle away from his body. He then viciously swipes counter-clockwise as if gutting an imaginary foe in front of him. The whole operation had taken a split-second. He bursts into devilish laughter as we cringe at the possibilities.

"*Calò', pi favure*. Stop it."

"Women!"

Happy at the macabre effect, he gently closes the knife, puts it away, and comes back to my birth.

"Okay, the story. Well, I saw the problem right away. The baby was halfway out, I could see his head and shoulders but I saw how tight the cord was around his neck."

He turns to Susan, "You know the cord. Right."

"Calogero, she knows, she's a woman."

"*Bedda madri*, I'm just checking. Anyway, it was strangling the little one…."

He looks at us to see if we are listening, and keeps his eye on me.

"Your mother gave one last push and you, *disgraziato,* finally came out. Your mother wanted nothing to do with you; she was screaming that you were dead, yes dead, not breathing, all blue and red of blood and gooey white stuff all over…."

He pauses, has a sip of his wine and repeats, "All bloody!"

This was a new story for me, and I couldn't even tell if he was making it up, which I am pretty sure he was.

"I saw this blue baby with the cord tied *seven times* around him, yes seven. I tried to slip the cord over the baby's shoulders. I pulled and stretched as much as I could but nothing worked. I told your aunt to hold the baby and I put a hot flame to this very knife…."

He takes out his knife one more time, opens it up, and acts out what he did.

"With this knife, disinfected as best as I could, I am not a doctor you know, me, yes a peasant, you didn't know that, this is the truth or God strike me down, me, I cut the cord between two knots, but it was too late, you were *dead*."

He bangs his glass on the table with that last word. He repeats the words, *too late*, and stops. Of course there was more.

He laughs and looks at the faces around the table, making sure he had hit the right note.

"I don't know how I thought of it, but I smacked you hard and you brayed like a donkey."

"You see everyone, I gave him life, nephew I gave you life, Susan, aren't you glad he lived?"

"Yes… Well maybe… Some days more than others." They both laugh. *Zia* joins in. Charlie and I smile weakly.

*Zio* keeps pouring wine, and after a while the alcohol begins to numb my senses. Sure, he tells everyone how he saved my life but he doesn't tell them how he ruined it.

Behind my uncle, at the entrance to his bedroom, I see my mother in her nightgown, no longer in bed but standing, looking at me, wanting to say something, appearing to wait for the opportune moment to interrupt. And then, as if in a hurry, while everyone else is talking, she blurts out, *"Son, you have to stop blaming your uncle. You have to put this thing behind you."*

I look at Susan, but before I can say anything, my mother is gone.

Her apparition is only slightly stranger than the fact that she endearingly called me son in a way that I had never heard her say it while she was alive. She also defended uncle, another thing I don't ever remember her doing.

Charlie gets up to help his mother clear the table and knocks over Susan's newly refilled glass. The wine spills on the table and makes a nasty red stain on the white table cloth while the glass rolls to the edge and, before I can catch it, falls to the stone floor breaking into a thousand pieces.

"*Porco cane*, you can't do anything right can you, how hard is it, picking up a dish. *Chi cazzu d'omo si?*" He raises his cane and yells at Charlie while questioning his son's manhood.

Susan and I jump to Charlie's defence.

"It's an accident," we both say.

Susan adds, "*Zio*, it is my fault, I moved the glass too close to the edge."

Everyone stops talking and we look at my uncle.

He makes us wait.

"Okay, okay, everybody relax, I'm not going to kill anyone. Charlie, just make sure you get every little piece. That's all I need, to get glass in my foot. *Porco cane!*"

Susan asks my uncle to tell us more, because she is interested and also to take the heat off Charlie.

"Okay, okay. Spilling wine is good luck. Susan, let me tell you, Salvatore's mother was a saint."

He says that, when my dad was away, and he was away a lot, it was he who took care of us. He shared the nothing he had with my mother and me. He gave us the storage loft to sleep in when we had nowhere to go.

"Your father, may he rest in peace, was always on the move. Before his army service, where he met your mother, he worked in Libya, you know, in Africa. He liked it there better than here. I don't know why. You want to know what I think. He was a bit crazy, maybe the African sun got to him, and I am his brother, I can say that. We farmers understand the land, the roots, family. Not your father. I don't know what he was looking for. I am not a doctor of the head but I say he was a bit touched."

It does not feel right to have my father attacked by his brother but I also know that it was true.

"What did he do in Libya?" Susan asks.

I knew the answer to that question.

"He worked in an olive oil factory." I turn to my uncle, "But *zio* didn't my father send money from Tripoli to pay for rent and food?"

"Oh yes, but you know it was so little."

My father always said that he kept just enough for him to eat and sent the rest to his brother and to his wife.

"I am sure he was trying to do the best for his family." Susan defends my father, and I resent her for it. He did not do what was best for me, or for my mother. He left us here, with uncle, for long periods of time, and I resented him for that.

"All I can say is that your mother was not like your father. She did not want to go to Africa, she liked it here in Italy, even if there was poverty. That's why she never joined him there in Tripoli, even though he wanted her to."

He says that my mother and my father were very different but I am not sure that they were all that different. In Canada, they acted the same way, dispassionate and superficial. They fed me, clothed me and sheltered me, but they gave me very little else, and it still hurts.

It was a mistake coming back; I didn't want to re-open those wounds.

"Charlie, take them to the cemetery. Show them the grave of your grandfather. Now there was a real man, what balls that cranky old man had. The stories I could tell you… Well, another day."

He waves us off, "Go, go."

As if staying here a moment longer will anger him to no end, and we wouldn't want to do that.

As I pass him, he grabs my arm and motions me with a small hand-wave to wait, and whispers, "I have something to say."

He waits for the others to get outside, and I feel old pangs of anxiety surface while I wait to see what cruelty he has in store for me. It was never a good thing to be taken aside by uncle.

He takes the curved knife out of his pocket.

"Your father refused this blade when your *nonno* offered it to him, to pass it on, you understand, your father was the eldest, it was for him. But, he didn't want the knife, thought that it had the *malocchio*, that it was bad luck. What an insult to our father, a real disgrace. Papa never forgave him. Your father did not understand; he was strange in that way. But, it is right that the knife belongs to you. Traditions are important to keep. I have made up my mind. Here, the knife, *she is yours*."

# FOUR

OUTSIDE, AN INTENSE scorching stillness bakes our quiet walk. It is the burning, reflective, white heat that I grudgingly admit I have missed. At each corner I expect to see my mother or maybe my father, and although I look for them, they or their ghosts are nowhere to be seen.

We cross Piazza Vittorio Emanuele and find ourselves in the centre of town, and across from the 14th century cathedral called La Chiesa Madre. My mother and I attended church there; it was also where Charlie had his confirmation. I look around and remember how Petra is an almost perfect equilateral triangle whose geographical and mathematical oddity no one has ever been able to explain except through various myths.

We take a small street flanked by houses stacked on top of each other. The town is deserted as people are having their post-meal naps, and Charlie quickens his step so that he can turn around to face us.

"Cousins, do you think people can just get up and leave a place, without wanting to come back, and things will be okay? Like your father did, Sal."

Susan answers a bit too quickly, "Yes, oh but it is something only you can answer. What do you think Sal?"

"I don't know."

I did know. I think people always know when the right time to leave comes. What Charlie really wants to know is if he can leave without hurting people and the answer is no. Someone always gets hurt. I keep those thoughts to myself, the way I keep most things to myself; Susan is right, I keep too many things inside. What am I afraid of, she's asked many times.

I let Susan and Charlie discuss the topic in emotional earnestness, and I am okay with that.

We continue our walk, and when there is a lull in the conversation I point to Susan the inner city gang-tags and political slogans that are spray-painted in black and in red on old Carthaginian walls.

"What a shame."

The vandalism and outward anger seem out of place in this sleepy town.

Most of the houses, built and re-built hundreds of years ago, are made of uneven, yellowish sandstone blocks held together by swatches of thick coarse mortar and plastered with harsh stucco that is in various degrees of disrepair and crumbling. Here and there, a new construction has replaced an old building, and a dull gold or pink-salmon veneer sticks out like fresh lipstick on a wrinkled face.

We smell lingering lunch-hour aromas, and to my surprise it is quite pleasant. The old part of the town is an Arab kasbah, a labyrinth of small streets, and of houses with inner courtyards where tables and chairs are set, and where day-to-day living takes place. Here and there an elderly man sits on a wooden chair, vacantly staring outwards, but otherwise the streets are empty. These courtyards offer the townspeople a double protection, from outsiders and from themselves.

Some of the abandoned properties have collapsed and the ruins have been left where they have fallen.

Draped in a black sack of a dress, a short and stout shadow glides out of a vaulted entrance. Head covered, dressed in mourning, she comes closer and casts a suspicious look at Susan and me, before recognizing Charlie. She offers us a weak smile reserved for strangers who are not perceived as dangerous but as intruding.

"*Sa benedica.*" Charlie gives the older woman the traditional respectful greeting that is both a blessing and a salutation.

"*Sa benedica,*" we echo in our best Sicilian.

The woman nods politely, appreciates the respect but is not overly welcoming, and walks away.

We turn down a miniscule street that, like most in this Arab medina, appears to begin and end nowhere, navigable only by the locals. Susan looks at me.

"Petra is such a quaint place. There is so much history... And a little piece of North Africa here... I had no idea. Sal, why for the love of God have you never said anything?"

I don't answer. Partly because that's the way I am, and partly because of circumstances. As a kid, I had blinkers on and I wasn't aware of history or of culture. The past was just stories that people told, and when I left, I forgot them. What I was seeing as an adult, for the most part, was as new to me as it was to Susan.

"Well, cousin Susan, I must disagree. Petra is a sad, suffocating place, with bitter young people, and crusty old people waiting to die," Charlie blurts out.

We walk quietly and let him talk.

"I can't leave this town, and I don't want to stay. Like its name, Petra is a stone around my neck...."

Charlie continues in a monotone, showing us the homes of distant relatives. He exposes markers of past memories, names I remember and others I don't.

"It's so boring here. There is no work, no clubs. There is nothing to do, every day is the same. I want to see the world but I am trapped...."

Charlie takes us through a serpentine and constricted side street toward a bar called *La cantina*, at the edge of a small Piazza. There is garbage everywhere. Susan asks Charlie about it and he says that Sicilian women spend hours cleaning and washing their houses and the dirt entrances to them, but think nothing of throwing their trash across the street into a semi-vacant lot or into a little-used common space. The wind does the rest. The people seem to have little sense of civic duty; and many, northerners in particular, attribute Sicily's poverty to that character flaw.

We step up into the café, and part the colourful plastic strips hanging in lieu of a front door.

"Ciao Charlie."

The young man behind the bar comes over to our side and kisses Charlie once on each cheek.

"These are my cousins from Canada."

Ciccio kisses our cheeks.

"*Piacere, benvenuti.* I am honoured to see you."

Ciccio has large wide-open, smiling eyes that immediately make us feel at home. He serves ice-cold Coca Cola for Charlie and me, and a fizzy orange drink for Susan. Here Charlie seems finally at ease, almost relaxed.

I try to pay but Charlie pulls my hand away and Ciccio says, "Your money is no good here, and neither is yours Charlie."

We chat a bit about my parents, he didn't know them; about Sicily, it's so beautiful here; and about Canada, it's mostly cold there. We exchange names of people we know or have heard of, smiling and nodding when a connection is made. Like Charlie, he talks with his hands.

"Ciccio is the dear friend who lent me the car."

We thank him for his generosity and he appreciates it.

"And if you're ever in Toronto, just let us know," adds Susan.

As we leave, I catch Ciccio handing Charlie a small package that he quickly shoves in his pocket. He also motions or signals to Charlie by twirling his index finger, making the Sicilian gesture for 'I'll see you later' while Charlie just raises his shoulders showing that he isn't sure.

Back on the sidewalk we cross the piazza, and go towards the Quartieri Spagnolo. Above our heads, laundry ropes, like umbilical cords, cross opposite wrought iron balconies tying the houses to each other, making them accomplices. As a child, I hadn't paid attention, but now taller, I notice how labyrinth-like the town really is, and inexplicably, this Arab construction feels like a home I should have known better.

Via Madona delle Carmine, a wide road built for mournful cortèges, takes us to the cemetery and away from the eastern tip of the town. The people of Petra buried their dead outside of the town's walls. It was their futile attempt to minimize the spread of disease and to ostracize death.

Again, as in the entrance to the town, tall pine trees, with white painted trunks, stand guard, except that here, as if waiting for my return, they remind me of my grandfather's funeral and my first visit to the city of the dead.

ଓ

… I follow a horse-drawn carriage carrying my grandfather's coffin, a procession that slowly winds its way towards the gates of the cemetery; a long line of mourners is behind us. The women in black with thin shawls covering their heads are screaming and wailing, telling my grandfather Salvatore what to do once he gets to the other side. They give him specific directives.

"When you see Luigi, tell him that I miss him."

"Say hi to my cousin Liboria."

"Tell Francesco, if he's there by mistake, that I wish he burns in hell, that son of a bitch."

"Find my brother and tell him his daughter is getting married to the butcher."

They hurl missives, laments and messages that even I as a six year old boy find ridiculous.

Almost as one, in need to catch their breath, they suddenly stop, crafting an eerie silence punctuated by the clip-clop of the horse's hoofs hitting the cobblestones and the incessant sound of crickets.

Frightened by the silence, I stare at these strange people, when abruptly and in unison, they return to yelling out their sadness for all of Petra and Sicily down below to hear. I now find their screams reassuring. The mourners compete against each other as to who can be the loudest, as if the higher the volume, the higher the sadness, and the more likely that the dead man will hear their howls and carry with him their precious words as his soul ascends towards heaven.

It is a good day, and I am happy.

I am laughing, running ahead of the cortège. I stop. I pick up the odd white rose that drops off the wagon, pluck its petals, toss it to the side and then return to my place. A woman I don't know tries to no avail to control my childish exuberance. I won't let her and sidestep her extended hand. I even receive a light slap to the back of my head thanks to uncle Calogero as I whiz by him.

I am happy this morning, not because my grandfather Salvatore died two days ago, but because my father has come back to Petra and is beside me, holding my hand when I am not running around.

The long procession stops.

Stiff and sombre, people gather around the coffin; my grandfather is lifted and gently deposited in his resting place on the second row of a mausoleum corner reserved for the Corbo family. I hear my dad sob, the one and only time, when the plaque is noisily screwed in place.

Later that night my father goes back to ignoring me, and spends the evening drinking and arguing with his brother. Loud and visceral insults are flying back and forth, mostly from my uncle. They talk of money, of Libya, of abandonment, of inheritance, of parcels of lands, and of almonds that are sold by the kilo but that no one wants. I wait for him to come and kiss me goodnight and tell me about the desert, but he doesn't and I fall asleep.

The next morning, he pinches my cheek, and asks me to be a good boy while he is away. With one hand, he ruffles my hair in lieu of a hug and I resent this touch that means he is leaving again.

ɷ

I try to conjure my father by whispering, "Why were you always going away? Why didn't you stay? Didn't you like me?" But, unlike my mother's ghost, when I call him, he doesn't show up.

My cousin leads us to the area where grandfather Salvatore and his family are buried. Ostentatious family crypts, tall and wide, with names like Ennio Flaiano and Tonino Guerra, flank the dirt pathway.

Lizards of all sizes with tails of varying length are scuttling about. I have always had a love-hate relationship with them. An adventurous lizard comes close, and Susan stops to admire him. I kick at him and he scurries away. Susan looks at me as if saying, what is wrong with you.

The cemetery is a maze of dirt walkways, a serpentine pattern not unlike that of the town.

Some of the family crypts look like chapels and diminutive cathedrals and have underground rooms for additional space.

"Look at that one, it must have cost their family a fortune."

One can't help but read tombstones in a cemetery, and I do so with a morbid curiosity. Antonio Pietrangeli was born and died in the same month. Mario Alicata was born and died on the twenty-eighth. Clara Fillipazzo just died.

After years of being steeped in English-Canadian culture, such an abundance of Italian names is an unexpected, but not unpleasant, culture shock.

We take a small pathway and finally get to the Corbo family plaque, in an older and poorer part of the cemetery. The

Corbo people don't have a building for their dead. Their families are stored and displayed on one long, above-ground wall. We stand in front of black and white photographs.

Susan does the sign of the cross and mouths the words of a prayer. I stand beside her, looking solemn, trying to remember what grandpa was like when alive, but, unable to do so, I simply stare at the picture, put my hand in my pocket and make a fist around the knife he once held. Surprisingly, it feels good to have that connection. I imagine grandpa smiling at the thought of me having his knife.

From behind us there is a noise and loud giggling. Charlie tenses up, cocks his head, stops talking, and tries to hear where the laughter is coming from.

"I'll be right back, I want to check something." Charlie quickly backtracks and zigzags to where we had been.

There are more sarcastic guffaws coming from near the entrance.

While waiting for Charlie, I scrutinize the pictures of women with well-rounded cheeks, and men with thick black moustaches wearing bowler hats.

There is more laughing and someone screams, "*Finocchio.*"

"What's going on?" Asks Susan.

"*Andate a fare tutti 'n culo. Bastardi. Figli di buttana.*"

I hear Charlie yelling profanities.

"Stay here," I tell Susan.

I take off for where I hear the voices, and see Charlie chasing three older teens. He stops, picks up a stone, threatening to throw it at them. The teenagers also stop, glare at him, dare him and then mock him.

He screams, "I know who you are and I know your parents, you are going to pay for this."

The hoodlums taunt him, goad him to fight back, and say that he should go fuck himself. They start walking menacingly towards him, repeat the word *finocchio*, slang for gay.

He sees me, looks embarrassed, unsure of himself, not knowing what to do.

I instinctively take my grandfather's knife out of my pocket and open it up the way my uncle showed us. Half-hidden I let it dangle to my side.

"Charlie, what's going on?"

They continue to walk towards us.

"Look... The bastards... My friend's grave..." he says haltingly, pointing to a mausoleum plaque that had been desecrated by graffiti.

Charlie is panting, out-of-breath scared, nervous, angry, somewhere between crying and screaming.

The boys now include me in their chant, "Faggots... Faggots... Faggots."

"Charlie, wait here."

I start walking towards the teens, followed closely by Charlie. I answer their taunts.

I yell words I remember my grandfather and my uncle using when they were really angry. I also add a few of my own.

"If I catch you, I'll cut your balls off and shove them down your throats so far down that you won't know what hit you, sons of bitches," and I flash my blade.

I throw Sicilian insults that come easily, and I point out in the Petran of my grandfather that it would only be the beginning of what I will do to them.

"I'll stick this blade so far up your assholes that you'll never be able to take a shit except through a tube, you fucking lizard-faced scum *bastardi*."

They stand their ground for one more moment, unsure if I'm bluffing, probably wondering if they can take us on.

Blood rushes to my head.

"Stinking bags of shit. I'm coming for all three of you." I scream and rush towards where they are standing, waving my knife like a wild man, and suddenly, truly frightened, no longer laughing, fearing for their lives, the young ruffians run off.

I continue screaming at them, "Do you know who I am? I'm the grandson of Salvatore Corbo; you don't want to mess with me, you puking miserable fucks. And, if you ever bother Charlie again…."

Susan arrives to see me stop running. Wheezing, I catch my breath and put the knife away.

"What happened here, sounded like World War III?"

Charlie shows her the soiled mausoleum plaque; "*Finocchio*" is scrawled diagonally in red paint. The tomb is that of Domenico Scala.

"He was my best friend. Look. Look what they did."

Charlie stands back, looks at his friend's picture and swallows hard.

"I am sorry," we both say.

Susan didn't even seem to mind my outburst, and although worried, she appreciated my defence of Charlie, my feistiness, as she called it. We go closer and see on the headstone the picture of a handsome young man, with delicate features, frail, not unlike Charlie's. The two could have been brothers. The date on the marble said that he died February 12, two years ago. He was born August 14, 1980.

"How did he die, an accident?"

"No, he was sick. The bad illness; the *Sida*, you know, Aids."

I am sorry for Charlie and his friend, but all I can think of is how alive I had felt a few moments earlier.

# FIVE

UNCLE CALOGERO HAS our evening planned out.

La Pentolccia, the eatery he has chosen for us, is about fifty yards from the foot of Castle San Michele and a long walk from his house. He moves briskly, swinging his cane and talking to Susan. *Zia* listens to them while Charlie and I keep a few steps back without saying a word. I am not sure what Charlie is thinking but I can't shake that earlier feeling of fear and excitement I hadn't felt since I was a child.

The restaurant is no more than a small but quaint wooden building and a dirt patio. A plume of grey smoke rises above an outdoor oven and dissipates towards Africa. Oversized burgundy umbrellas and plastic tables flank a low-rise imitation Punic wall that overlooks a jagged cliff and the Mediterranean below. Susan is impressed; I knew this place before it was a restaurant and wonder why uncle chose to bring us here.

The thick trunk of a majestic fig tree is the centrepiece of this terrace. Its intertwined branches, now thicker than I remember, hang over the bucolic yard, forming a canopy of wide leaves.

When I was younger, this place was deserted, abandoned to weeds and lizards, but this is the same recognizable tree that I climbed as a child, a tree full of succulent black figs.

I remember sitting on those branches above our heads. There I would pluck the oversized teardrop fruit and let the sticky milky stem-sap run to its side. I had my own way of eating figs. I peeled away the rubbery brownish nibs and some of the attached skin. Holding it with two hands, thumbs dipping into its sweetness, I'd pry the fig in two. Fingering for a brief moment the moistness of the fig's inner parts, I'd lick the red meat crisscrossed by crimson filaments, feeling its ripeness with my tongue, before putting one half into my mouth. I remember the ritual; I would not bite into it but would let my tongue squeeze the honeyed innards against the roof of my mouth before swallowing whole. I'd then do the same to the other half, licking my lips when it was over. I've never tasted figs like that since then.

I have a strong sensory memory of small arms and legs hooked on the top branches of this gargantuan tree planted in mediaeval times. Hanging precariously, I could see the town of Petra and beyond it. I imagined I saw Cap Bon on the African coastline, in Tunisia, where the seeds of this tree had originated, according to my father. He had also played here as a child and had shown me many of the castle's hiding places.

I wonder if Charlie had ever climbed this tree. Probably not, since he seems more interested in his cell phone, which he keeps checking.

"You know what figs mean?" Uncle asks Susan, knowing quite well that he is crossing into salacious territory.

"No, what?"

Susan falls into his trap. She doesn't know what we all know, and it makes it the more embarrassing.

He smirks, "It means, you know, the woman... Her sex... Her *figa*."

She finally gets it, blushes and then giggles.

"It's because of how it looks, when you break it in half," he adds, as if needing to explain, "and how it feels. Moist, you know... I hope it does not embarrass you but young men would dream, and... You know, you know...." And I imagine or actually see him do a small thrusting motion to emphasize the imagery.

Belatedly, *zia* scolds her husband, and pretending innocence, he shouts, "What did I say? Sex is natural, some boys even used the small ripe yellow melons that we...."

"*Ma, Calò....*"

"Okay, *porca la miseria,* one can't say nothing anymore, it's what young men do. *Bedda Madir, testa ca non parla si chiama cucuzza!*"

Susan asks me to translate and I tell her that it just means that a non-talking head is just a zucchini. Uncle waits for me to finish the translation, and laughs heartily at what he thinks is great wit.

Susan also laughs and it just encourages him.

"But I must tell you, they had a temple for Venus, right where the castle is now, and people there had sex all the time, men, women, and even with animals...."

"*Calò....*"

"*Pa....*"

He can't let it go. He loves the attention and the uproar he's causing.

"Susan, Sal, did you know that in Greek time this town was one big bordello, and then Zeus got mad at what was going on, took out his big sword and lobbed off the top of the mountain, that's why the town is like a slice of cheese."

*Zia* agrees with her husband. She says that they were taught about the Greeks when she was in school.

"Mother you are confusing things, those are myths."

Uncle continues.

"No, it's the truth, Hercules came to this island, angered the Sicilians, and then the Sicilians tried to steal his sacred cow, and he became so angry that he cursed us with eternal poverty. Because before that Sicily was rich, the breadbasket of the Mediterranean it was."

"Father, you don't know what you are saying. Cousins, you see the ignorance."

"And you do? You, look at him people, the great, educated man who didn't finish school. *Si na testa di rapa.*"

He calls Charlie a turnip head, in effect a blockhead, and *that* Susan understands.

Antonio is the owner of the restaurant, as well as our greeter and server. His interruption is welcomed; uncle had that look he used to get before exploding. Antonio says that his wife is the number one cook in the whole province and that we are in for a treat.

Hyperboles were also a Sicilian trait I had difficulty reconciling with.

Cousin Charlie isn't saying much; he seems preoccupied, more anxious than ever. The events at the cemetery had shaken all of us but he had made Susan and me promise not to say anything to his father. Charlie keeps looking at the small screen on his phone.

"I hope you're hungry," *Zio* says in a tone implying that to think otherwise would be a mortal insult. I remember that tone, had it tattooed in my mind. It was the same tone that he used when he would hiss, "I hope you finished your chores... I hope you weren't thinking of eating that cookie... I hope you did not rip your Sunday pants... I hope it wasn't you throwing those stones," a tone that implied that the answer to his question had better be a resounding yes; and when the answer wasn't yes, it was a tone that meant, you'd better brace yourself for a slap to the back of the head.

Antonio, in his role of friend and waiter/owner, discusses with uncle the politics of the day, family, and what we are going to eat, all in the same sentence. The effusive little man flings his hands about as he describes each plate, making sure we understand that his precious wife will even skin a rabbit if we so desire, to which Susan responds with a quick, "No thank you!"

*Zio* laughs and keeps looking at Susan's breasts, whose curves are showing themselves more than usual from within the low-cut sundress she is wearing. It is stupid of me to feel jealousy, but I know the old man is flirting with Susan, ogling her, and yes *I am* jealous. Jealousy is a feeling I am not used to, but today, here in this town, I feel it. I also remember him looking at my mother in the same way, and at that memory my stomach tightens.

"May I bring you to drink while you observe at the menu," Antonio says, proudly showing off his broken English.

Uncle orders us a liter of the best red wine Trapani has to offer, and with Antonio agrees that an antipasto platter is an excellent idea to start us off.

Charlie adds a tall bottle of mineral water, "*Naturale, per favore, Antonio.*"

Antonio scurries away and we look at the menu, pointing out the interesting and unusual Sicilian dishes.

"Couscous in Sicily? I'm so surprised, they even have sweet couscous," says Susan.

*Zia* tells Susan that *Cuscusu Trapanese* is famous throughout the world. She is exaggerating, but for some reason I also had disassociated Arab couscous from the *cuscusu* that was served in Petra when I was a child. I try to sort out what I thought I remembered from what I see in front of me. Everything is blurring, morphing, and I don't like it.

"It comes from the *Negroes*." Uncle elaborates.

"North African Arabs… Actually it's a Berber dish," explains Charlie.

Uncle bristles at the rebuke.

"*Zitto stronzo*! Africans, Arabs, *Marocchino*. It's all the same, and *please*, don't contradict me in front of company."

My aunt tells us how couscous is prepared. She delights in telling us that the fish is sautéed in a large casserole with garlic and onions, and you add parsley and cover with tomatoes and then let it simmer. Her eyes light up with excitement.

"Then that's what I am having," Susan says.

"I'll have *Cavatelli alla Norma*."

I'm not a fussy eater. As a child I used to enjoy eating, everyone said that, but after we left Sicily I lost my sense of taste. These days, I find eating to be just functional; something that one does quickly so as to not waste time. Susan has always hated my eating habits and I know she's right, but I can't help myself, I just pretend more when she's around.

Charlie closes the menu.

"*Non ho fame, stasera. Non mangio.*"

He says he's not hungry.

Uncle looks at him as if his best friend had stabbed him, his eyes bulge, a deadly seriousness comes over his face, the one that says I am no longer kidding. The one that says I gave birth to you and I can take it away. That's how I remember him; coiled, ready to snap at a moment's notice. My heart stops.

"Tonight you will eat, and if you can't order for yourself I will order for you. You don't insult me, or my guests or *compare* Antonio. Never!"

He shakes his finger, not up and down but slicing side to side emphasizing his words. "Never, you understand?" He makes a motion with his cane.

The words freeze everyone into submission, into silence.

I say nothing. I remember that look. Hadn't seen it for over thirty years, but it is not one you forget. *Zio* could neutralize and impale you with that stare.

Susan defends Charlie.

"*Zio*, it's not an insult to us. I am so happy to be here. You have chosen such a beautiful restaurant and such a beautiful place; everything is perfect. Let's not spoil the evening."

Uncle mellows. He brushes her thigh and says, "*Bene*, for you I do it, but my father was right when he used to say, *he who has children has devils.*"

Even Susan' diplomacy annoys me. There was no one to mellow uncle when he used to let *me* have it. No one stopped him from making me feel like I was a useless inconvenience to him. No one stopped him from giving me the belt. Unlike Susan, my mother just stood by.

Charlie discreetly fingers his cell phone and *text messages* while his father chats with Susan.

Thankfully, Antonio is back quickly, bringing a bottle of Nero D'Avola and five glasses. I can use the drink.

"It's the best wine in Trapani."

Uncle grabs the bottle from him, examines it as if he was a knowledgeable sommelier, and expertly pours a glassful for each of us. He orders another bottle of wine and proposes a toast.

"To my nephew and his beautiful wife. To family! To being together!"

We cheer, and clink glasses. *Zio* is happy again.

The wine is most welcome.

I saw posters advertising the feast of San Calogero and I ask if they are looking forward to it.

"You just missed it. It was last weekend."

I tell Susan that San Calogero is the patron saint of Petra.

Uncle adds, "San Calogero is loved by everyone, a good little black man."

"Black man?"

I am also surprised, but I am glad that it is Susan who is asking because I had forgotten that San Calogero was a black icon, not unlike the black Madonna.

"*Sì*, a little *negreto*, my namesake, who grants wishes to believers."

Charlie tears himself away from his phone and joins the conversation. "Cousin Susan, it's one of those charming aspects of Sicilians, that they can be racist against Africans, Arabs, that they can hate everyone who is not a relative or from their hometown, and then go out and worship a black man."

"Son, you're being blasphemous."

"No father, you see a black man and you hold on to your wallet, mommy sees a black man and crosses the street, Sicily sees a black man and pegs him for a diseased trinket seller on the beach, and half of Petra would love to send all Arabs to Africa, and then Petrans turn around and adore a black saint...."

"*Basta.* Stop. You've said enough. Nephew, niece, don't believe *quello stupido.* In the morning of the feast day we buy blessed bread. The whole town smells of fresh bread. We line up to see the saint leave the church and offer him the bread."

Charlie will not let go. "You see, cousins, they call all Africans *marocchini*, people from Morocco, not withstanding where they come from, blacks, Arabs, they are all the same to Sicilians. They don't bother learning about them as people. God forbid a Sicilian woman who falls in love with an African."

*Zia* strategically goes back to San Calogero. "He was made a saint because he collected bread for the poor and took it to the lepers, that's why we throw bread at him."

Charlie does not give up and I like his tenacity.

"Yes, cousins, throw bread. The truth is that they were afraid to touch him so they threw the bread at him instead of handing it to him... And even more disgusting, after the feast, all you see is this trampled *blessed* bread on the streets, being collected and thrown in the garbage. *That,* dear cousins, is the feast of San Calogero. I never go."

"*Sei un stronzo.* He is a good saint." His father says while aunt adds, "*Chiarlie,* you exaggerate."

I want to see where this is going, but Susan does not want any of this argument.

She says, "*Zio*, tell me more about Salvatore. He," Susan points to me and accuses, "*He* won't tell me anything about himself. He's Mr. Secret, keeps everything to himself. That's why I dragged him back here. What about his father, and his mother? They passed away before I met Sal."

"Ha! His mother, that is another story, an angel, another saint, I tell you, a beautiful woman. After her wedding, she stayed here in Petra, cut off from her family in Calabria."

"Why?"

"Her family, *quei miserabili*, pig-headed *calabresi*, excuse my language, disowned her. It was a major disgrace. You see, my brother was a soldier, doing his military, stationed there, you know. I'm sure Salvatore told you the story."

"No!"

"There was no story," I say.

"Oh! Yes there was. Your father had to marry your mother. You know she was in the family way with you."

He spews this lie as if it was common truth.

"*Zio*, you're exaggerating."

The drinking must have finally gotten to him. Neither my mother nor father ever said anything about this.

"Ask your aunt, as God is my witness, I'm telling you the truth."

She says, "It's true, Totò."

I can't believe what they are saying. My mother should appear now and set them straight.

He turns to Susan.

"My brother did the honest thing. They had to marry. Her parents, ignorant people, hated your father, they thought she was marrying beneath her. Her family were merchants, they owned a fruit stand, big deal, and we were farmers, at least we were honest. Her father never spoke to his daughter again. Her own mother had to sneak around to see her. She was young. I took care of you two, especially when my brother was away."

"The poor woman. That was so generous of you. What a sad story!" Susan says. "Sal, your parents, I had no idea…."

I am half-listening, still shocked, looking for my mother to show up. To tell me that it wasn't true. I didn't know any of this. What is true is that I don't have good memories of my parents.

My mother passed away a year after my father died of lung cancer. I was not happy, but I wasn't as sad as I thought I would be. I didn't cry at either funeral. My mother got melanoma; it started as a cold and ended up as cancer. I felt nothing, unsure to this day if it was stoicism or indifference. Her death freed me from having to make an effort to be nice to her after my father died, to pretend that I had loved her while she was alive, before she got sick. My relationship with her died long before she did. I don't think she ever knew what to do with me. She was never meant to be a mother, now I see why. My birth must have ruined her life and trapped my father, until he started running away. I don't ever remember a hug or a kind word from her. She never said she loved me; why would I have loved her back. Maybe she didn't want to get married either, maybe she didn't like what her life had become, but it wasn't my fault. I didn't ask to be born, but she made it seem like I was to blame. My uncle should have let me die at birth.

Susan squeezes my hand, as if she can read my thoughts, and for the first time in a long while I feel like crying, something I haven't done since I left Sicily. I welcome Susan's hand; I feel a new softness in the touch of her fingertips.

The conversation switches to the townspeople and relatives I barely remember and it exasperates me. I shouldn't have let Susan convince me to come back here for a holiday. I had a half-idea that it would help me, but I was wrong, I was only reliving what I had wanted to forget.

Charlie isn't saying anything. *Zia* isn't very talkative either. The only two that seem to enjoy themselves are uncle and Susan, they begin a goofy banter about green almonds, edible before they mature, and which people say make men more virile, and women even sexier. They are both drinking a lot.

Charlie continues to *message* under the table.

Antonio, balancing an oversized platter, interrupts us. He sets on the table a buffet-like antipasto tray and we begin filling our plates; even Charlie can't resist a few olives and a slice of bread, which he dips in an olive oil, balsamic vinegar and black pepper concoction he has poured on his plate. I watch how *Zia* eats. She gently smells her food, approves with a nod and begins, slowly, almost sensually, to put each morsel in her mouth, waits a bit more, fully enjoying the pleasure of the moment, and then starts again. She is in charge of her senses and it surprises me. She seems more sensory than I am. Snobbishly, I hadn't thought her capable.

Uncle is anxious to pick up from where he left off.

"His mother would help us as much as she could. She would bring us our noonday meal, especially when we worked the nearby fields, the ones I owned. She was a strong woman, very proud, and did I say, very beautiful, she had the seven beauties, very rare, a real catch for my brother."

I shouldn't be, but I am surprised at his bluntness, seven beauties is the highest compliment a Sicilian can give.

ଓ

I see my mother packing dense Sicilian bread, not unlike the type we are eating at this moment, as well as thick hand-cut slices of greasy *pancetta* and pink fatty *mortadella*. She throws in triangles of strong black pepper cheese, the same pieces of *Crotone* that decorate the hors d'oeuvre plate brought to the table by a sweating and red-faced Antonio. Same food, different time. The strong smells waking my taste buds also bring back more memories.

... She includes deeply grooved and oversized, red tomatoes as well as short, bloated light-green cucumbers called *cetrioli* to the mix and deposits the whole lunch into a tablecloth, tying the four corners into a knot. Mother takes with her a large terracotta jug of water and a smaller one full of homemade wine. The water jug is perched on her head, anchored there by a simple cloth towel made into a crown. It is a daily routine. We bring the workers their food and then come back to the town. Once back inside the Gates of Trapani, she buys me flavoured ice. The merchant grates it from a block of ice, which he carries in a wheelbarrow, ice covered by cheesecloth to keep it from melting.

"Mama, why do you bring them food?"

"I do my part."

I am also expected to do simple chores, like cleaning the stable, fetching the bread from the bakery and looking after the mule.

When I get older my mother asks that I stay home and finish my chores while she goes to the fields to deliver the workers their food....

I remember feeling hurt and rejected.

ଔ

"Totò, do you remember when you ran away and we couldn't find you. That was a strange day. Susana, did he ever tell you, do you want to hear *that* story? It's a good story."

He had changed Susan's name to Susana, a variation she is not fond of, but here, in Sicily, she lets him. He is charming her and she is falling for it.

"*P-lease*, he never says anything. He's a closed book, my Sal."

Calling me "My Sal" is a new one. She is adopting their syntax, their hyperboles and I don't like it.

"Susan, I was barely eleven before I left for Canada. I can't be expected to remember everything."

"*Oh please*. You just don't want to reveal anything about yourself."

Her laughter tells me that she wants me to believe she's just joking.

"Sal is so serious, he can't even tell when I'm kidding. Was he always like this?"

I am grateful for Antonio's stealth approach and ready-to-serve presence. He asks if we are ready to order. *Zio* orders for us. He says that we should pardon his presumption, that he knows better, and that unless we really object, he wants us to try *compare* Antonio's couscous. He orders the dish for all of us. He says that we can't leave Petra without tasting its most popular dish. He then, if we again don't mind, orders grilled tuna garnished with fennel for the whole table.

"It is better this way, we all have the same thing."

Charlie interrupts his father, "Antonio, no couscous, no tuna for me, just a *capriciosa* salad."

His father explodes.

"What's wrong with the couscous *I* ordered? You are too good for real Sicilian food; you want a *amburger di machdonaldo*, instead? Antonio do you have a *amburger*?"

"I don't want any couscous tonight. I'm allowed to choose my own food. I am not a baby."

"No, but you are ignorant and disrespectful."

Susan tries to be a peacemaker and change the subject, brings it back to me. "*Zio*… About Sal?"

I have another glass of wine.

"No, as a kid Totò was not serious. He was wild, always fooling around, playing alone in the castle or in this tree instead of doing his chores."

Climbing trees and being a lizard slayer was normal. I chased lizards and when I caught them I tortured them. They were my enemies, and I made it my goal to rid the castle of these reptiles. I knew every nook and cranny of this crumbling mess of a castle and every branch of this fig tree. I didn't want to share my world with anyone else, not then, not now. I was happy alone. The fight with the lizards was personal; the rest was normal child play.

"At first we forbade him to go to the castle or to climb the fig tree, but he kept coming here. Do you remember, Salvatore, how many times you got the belt for disobeying?"

He says it as if hitting a small child was normal, as if the welts they created on my skin were normal.

"Sometimes you have to prune the young branches, otherwise the tree won't grow strong and healthy," he explains in lieu of an apology.

Susan is annoying me. On one hand I can sense that she is repulsed by uncle's patriarchy, his explosive anger and controlling behaviour; on the other hand I see her indulging him, as if making a point about me, as if telling me that she enjoys the company of people who show their emotions either good or bad.

Charlie continues to look uninterested, like he would rather be anywhere but here.

"That day, around suppertime, when we came back from the fields, he was nowhere to be found."

# SIX

I AM STATIONED at my post, at the foot of the southern wall of my castle, reigning over a treacherous Kingdom, being attacked by poisonous green lizards; lizards that hold my father captive outside of Tripoli, where he is made to work in an olive oil factory. The tiny reptiles are everywhere. One of them, a fat one, slower than the others, finds his way into my right hand. I grab him, not by the tail, but by the neck, turn him over, hold him down, and place a rock on his bloated stomach. His lungs inflate and deflate, lifting the stone up and down as he tries to breathe and dislodge the stone. He won't live. I know the appropriate weight to put on a green lizard's stomach to make him suffer. The breathing gets more pronounced, then slows down, a last quick gasp, and I watch him die without guilt. I hate my uncle, and wish him to be under the stone.

I came here, to the castle, against my mother's wishes. She thinks that I am doing my chores. My father has abandoned me, and never comes home. At Christmas he brought me a small, useless plastic camel, a toy for a much younger child, and not the slingshot I asked for. At Easter he didn't bring me anything, and now it is the fall and he has been away a long time. It is *that* day that I decide to conquer my fears and to climb up to the highest point of the crumbling turret, the highest point of the castle. I have been warned not to go up there, that it is too dangerous, that I will get the belt if I disobey, but I want the danger, I can do anything I want, and if I fall and die I don't care. No one else does.

"He gave us such a scare, we couldn't find him."

The climb isn't easy but I know I can make it. I am afraid of falling, but, imitating the lizards, I wrap myself around the stone ledge and slowly crawl forward without looking down. I feel tense and excited, afraid and rebellious. I am the king of the lizards and I can do anything. I feel powerful.

I get to the peak, my mission is accomplished, the operation is a success, my scraped knees and slashed elbows are proud wounds, and the trickle of blood is a small price to pay for victory. I have climbed as high as I can go. I have conquered the castle. It is now mine. I'm king of the castle.

I am also running away from my uncle, never want to see him again.

Last night, *zio* should not have slapped me. All I said was, "You can't make me do that, you're not my father," and my mother should have yelled at him when I told her that he hit me. She didn't, then agreed with him that I was too rebellious, too much of a nuisance, and that I should be more respectful. She said that he was in charge while my father was away, and that obeying once in a while would not hurt me.

*Zio* continues with his story.

"I was working in the fields that day along with cousin Luigi and his two brothers; I hired them. It was almond season, a very busy time for all of us. That's when we made a few miserable *lire,* to live on."

I am no longer listening to him.

... I am on the turret at one corner of the castle, the one where the ramparts are still intact. Here, no one can see me. I can hide behind the crenulated wall and observe the whole town, the church, the piazza, *zio's* house and even the great metal iron gates that guard the entrance to Petra. I can also watch the port below us. More importantly, I can spy on the farmers, on the men who are working in the nearby fields. *Zio* and his crew are already there harvesting almonds. I can see them. If I yelled they would notice me, and possibly smile or wave, except that uncle would come over and kill me. With long wooden canes they hit the clusters of almonds, and shake the branches. When the whole tree is empty of its fruits, the men collect the small harvest and fill the bamboo baskets, before moving on.

I can see everything.

The mule and the cart they use to transport the almonds back into town are close to me, underneath the tower. From here I can also see the big boats leaving for Tunisia, I can see the blue water and I see what I think is the coast of Africa.

"We had just gotten home from the fields, dead tired, like overworked beasts, and were unloading the almonds, almonds we would shell later, when his mother ran towards us and asked if I had seen Totò on my way home. I told her I hadn't seen him all day, which was the truth, and that he probably would soon show up. I was not too worried. He was always getting into trouble." He tries to bring me into the story by pointing at me with his cane, but instead his story pushes me deeper into a past I had forgotten.

... My mother is walking along the small pathway to where the men are working. From above, I am tracking her route. It feels good and it feels bad to see and not be seen. From up here, everything appears smaller but there is more of it. She is bringing their lunch. Once they spot her, they greet her with respect, but they also joke with her in a familiar way. Uncle helps her with the heavy load and takes the first swig from the wine jug. His cousins take turns drinking and wiping their brows with the colourful handkerchiefs they have tied around their necks. He says something to her, close to her ear, and she laughs in a way I don't often see her laugh. She mouths a few words that I can't hear and they roar. They're all happy without me, and it makes me angrier. They would probably be happier without me, and I should just die.

She unties her long black hair and flicks it back. She spreads out the red striped tablecloth, the one she uses to bundle their lunch, and on it she unwraps their noonday meal.

Almost in unison, the workers take out their curved long knives, flick them open and use them to cut into the meats, the vegetables and the cheeses.

Below me, underneath the castle, the mule Rosetta is grazing, and I also watch her eat, which reminds me that I should be cleaning her stall, and that I will be in trouble once I get home. I don't care and take pleasure in the fact that I am disobeying uncle. Shaded, the mule is in a small alcove of trees and bushes hidden from where the men are working. Lazily, she swats flies away with her tail. Uncle's cart is lifted up and leaning against a tree.

A while later my mother is about to leave. Uncle yells that he needs to give Rosetta a drink and grabs the water jug.

"I saddled my mule and went looking for him. Everywhere I went I asked if they had seen little Totò and they all said, 'No'. We organized a search party with my *compare*. His mother, I must tell you, was as pale as the moon with worry, but I kept reassuring her that by the grace of San Calogero everything would be fine."

Our food arrives. The dinner talk becomes about how good it all looks and how big the portions are. I am grateful for the interruption and I hope he ends the tale here.

Charlie, distracted and uninterested, picks at his tomato salad. He might be, understandably so, still upset by the events at the cemetery. Or it may be about the messages he's secretly *texting* on his phone, under the table. *Zia* perpetually nods and smiles. Susan is taking it all in. The stories are more than she had hoped for. She was discovering the tales that I had hidden from her, but disturbingly they were changing my own memories of those events. Uncle was changing what I remembered.

"*Zio*, please continue. What happened to Sal?"

Uncle pours another round of wine and does not need much prompting to carry on.

"I decided to search near the castle. I told his mother I thought he might be near the ruins, probably having fallen asleep somewhere under the bushes. It was to keep her heart from breaking open in pain that I told her that. The first place I went to look for was right here."

He looks at Susan and she nods, eager to hear more.

"Was he here?"

... I can see my mother walking ahead. My uncle quickens his step while she slows hers. The distance between them gets shorter until the two are walking side by side. I spy on them. They stop. He picks up a flower and gives it to her. She slaps his arm when he tries to put it around her shoulder, and looks back to see if anyone saw them. They both laugh. He leans over and whispers something. He asks her to wait while he gives Rosetta a drink.

"I stood at this very spot, under the fig tree, and called, 'Totò, Totòooo', but there was no answer. I even climbed the tree to make sure *you*," he points at me, "were not playing hide and seek, or being difficult. As God is my witness, you were not an easy child to raise, what with your father always gone."

He stops talking long enough to take a bite of his grilled tuna, and to smack his lips. Everyone waits for him; they want to hear more. Even Charlie is now listening.

... My mother watches my uncle pour water from a jug into a wooden pail. He places it under Rosetta's head and stands back. The mule greedily laps up the water, pushing her long nose right into the bucket, bopping her head up and down, flaring her nostrils, unfurling her wide pink tongue and using it as a ladle to scoop up the water.

"Next, I went to the castle and again called your name as loud as I could. I even climbed that dangerous tower you were not allowed to go up on, in case you were stuck up there and had no way of coming down, but no luck. By San Calogero, you were nowhere to be found."

... My uncle goes to where my mother is standing watching him. Suddenly, he reaches and lifts up her long skirt, points to her exposed bare thighs, laughs and then lets it fall.

*"My son, you shouldn't have been watching, you shouldn't have been there."*

My mother's voice startles me. Sounding like she did before she got sick, the words come from behind me, but afraid to turn around and see her ghost, I just put my head down and pretend to eat.

Uncle continues, "I met up with the search party and still nothing. He had disappeared from the whole of Sicily, swallowed by the great African sea." He looks at us to make sure we appreciate the imagery, and takes another forkful of fish. He sees himself as a great storyteller.

... I look down from my tower, and uncle, standing at my mother's side, is stroking her long curls. He asks for a kiss, pointing to his cheek, and she kisses him. He asks for another one and when she leans towards him he turns his face so that her lips land on his. She leaves them there for a long time and it is disgusting. He squeezes her shoulders, drapes his arms around her and hugs her tightly, hurting her. She lets him hurt her and she doesn't fight back. He was being a bad man and she was letting him being bad. They said *I* was bad.

*"I must correct you my son, he was not hurting me, it was not like that at all, that is what men and women do sometimes. You should not have been spying on us. You should have been doing your chores."*

"I jumped back on the mule. I was now very worried. The postman said that they had seen a Moroccan merchant talking to you. Cousin Luigi went to the *carabinieri* to denounce him and have him arrested on the spot." Uncle bangs his plate to emphasize the gravity of his point, and Susan jumps. "On Rosetta, I rode out of the town's gate like a demon, I went to look for you and the Moroccan, thinking the worst. With my knife, I was ready to cut him into pieces."

Now I know he is lying, he never cared that much for me, and Rosetta never moved that fast.

I shouldn't be, and I can't see why, but I'm suddenly enjoying the strange taste of the grilled tuna and seared fennel going down my throat.

... My uncle kisses my mother's neck. She doesn't run away from him, because she can't. He is forcing her to stay. He disengages his hand from the embrace and lifts the skirt up above her underwear, and she doesn't yell or scream. I would have heard her. She lets him do whatever he wants. It is disgusting and I look away.

*"You don't understand, it wasn't disgusting. Maybe it was wrong, but not disgusting. You were too young to understand. I was alone; your father was always away. After you were born, he didn't want me, didn't want to touch me. Your uncle was...."*

"People were suggesting all kinds of crazy things. That you had been kidnapped, that you were going to be sold as a slave in Africa. I went towards Trapani, taking the short route. I was determined to find you, for your poor mother's sake, if nothing else."

... Unable to stay away, I sneak a peek from between the stones and see my uncle from behind my mother, gently pushing her towards the upturned wagon.

She is not saying anything and neither is he.

*"Your uncle may have been rough but how many times do I have to tell you that he didn't force me. You must stop blaming just him, don't forget there were others to blame."*

"I would ride a bit, get off, check the side of the road, but nothing. At this point, I thought that he might be dead somewhere on the side of a ditch and I thought how his poor mother would react to that news."

... My mother is now pinned against the cart by my uncle, whose pants have fallen down, and I continue to watch.

"I finally spotted you walking on the side of the road and I called your name. When you heard me, instead of stopping, instead of being glad to see me, you started running. I guess you knew you were in trouble. I got off the mule and started chasing after you."

... He detaches himself from her, and she pulls up her underwear and lowers her skirt.

"He was such a little wild animal. He didn't want to come back home. I had to give him a good one, on the back of the head. He then kicked me in the groin, that little son of a bitch. I lost it and smacked him hard, on the face. I never hit the face, but that time... He stopped fighting me and started crying. I put him on the mule, and tied him there like a sack of almonds."

... Her face is all red. She ties her dishevelled hair back using her handkerchief, and stands a few steps from uncle. He goes to her and violently kisses her on the lips.

*"My son, it wasn't violent. You must understand, your father was neglecting me, you couldn't have understood, it was complicated but it wasn't about you. I swear to you."*

"I tied him to the saddle, and walked beside Rosetta."

He fills his wine glass.

"But you know Susan, I love my nephew, I am glad I got him back before he got hurt. Can you imagine if he had made it to the port? He surely would have been stolen and taken to Africa. I saved his life, again."

... I move away from the rampart and lie against the inner wall of the ancient tower. I cry for a long time. The crying puts me to sleep, and when I wake, it is quite clear to me what I must do. I must go to my father, and never come back to Petra.

*"Is that why you have hated me for all those years?"*

"You were terrible that summer, you kept running away. You got the belt so many times, but it didn't stop you from being bad."

As a distraction, I drink more wine. She was right. I did stop talking to her and to uncle and to pretty well everyone else. I still don't feel like talking to anyone. She was right, I hated her, but she wasn't the only one I hated. She was wrong. It was about me; it was about being born at the wrong time, and in the wrong family.

About six months later my father came back and told my mother that we were moving to Canada, that he had been sponsored, and that the approval had just arrived. She didn't argue.

*"Do you not see that your father blamed me for getting pregnant with you, that he blamed me for ruining his life, for not wanting to go to Libya with him. He hated this damned town. He hated me."*

A phone rings and we all jump, having been in a kind of trance. Charlie gets up, searches his pockets, and retrieves his cell phone.

I want to ask my mother if my father knew, if it was the reason we left, but she's gone.

"*Pronto....*"

We look at Charlie as he leaves the table.

"*Porca la miseria, Sempre con quel miserable telefonino.*"

The old man explains to us that he is not so much angry at the use of the phone but that Charlie is always on it, and that it costs money, money he doesn't have, money that does not fall from the clouds.

Uncle drains his glass and grabs the bottle for a refill.

"Wasn't that a marvellous story. Wine is the milk of the aged, and I am old," he concludes as he takes another sip.

*Zio* smiles at Susan. He makes a grand gesture and orders dessert for us, Lemon *Granita* for everyone. The iced dessert served in a cup comes topped with a sprig of fresh mint.

Susan, who is a cheap drunk and whose legs turn to rubber after a glass of wine, is on her third tumbler and obviously much too comfortable. Charlie comes back to the table and you can see that his mind is elsewhere. He doesn't say whom the call is from and no one asks him. I notice his tattoo again and wonder about him, about his life here in Petra.

Abruptly, insensitive to the fact that his wife is in mid sentence with Susan, *zio* wipes his mouth and says, "This was wonderful, it had to be done. But now it's time to go."

As I see Antonio coming over, I get up and take out my credit card. He very politely informs me that the bill has been taken care off by my uncle.

"No, no… take my card," I say in forceful Sicilian.

"No, no, I can't, by orders of the *comandante*."

*Zio* has taken care of a bill he couldn't afford, and I don't want his generosity.

"It was supposed to be on us…"

*Zio* nods and says, "*Vai, è fatto, andiamo*. You are my guests."

His guest indeed. If I was a true Sicilian, I would get my grandfather's knife and slice him in half for what he did with my mother, for what he did to my father, and for how he messed up my life. But I had rejected my Sicilian blood a long time ago.

As we walk away from the castle, my mother comes up right beside me and whispers in my ear, "*It was you who told your father, admit it, and because of you we left Sicily, so stop blaming your uncle for ruining your life. If we must blame, think about how you ruined my life twice. It wasn't just about you...*"

I stop listening to her and she disappears.

ଓ

We return to their house. Uncle gives us his matrimonial bed, in the only bedroom of the house, and they take the sofa bed in the living room where Charlie usually sleeps. Susan makes a fuss, saying it isn't right and that she insists we take the sofa.

"No! I've decided. There will not be any discussions." He raises his voice and Susan acquiesces.

Charlie leaves and says that he will see us in the morning. He tells us he is staying at a friend's house.

"*Buona notte*," Uncle and aunt say at the same time.

"*Buona notte*," Susan answers, but, still angry, I say nothing.

An old porcelain doll in a frilly pink dress centres the bed we have been assigned, and I feel out of sorts. *Zia* told us that she changed the sheets when she found out that we were coming, a small consolation for what I'm feeling. I have not said a word since we left the restaurant, trying to make sense of what I heard and what I felt then and of what I remembered then and of what I feel now. It wasn't so much my mother's ghost that bothered me but that my memories were back-pedaling and confusing me. I don't remember telling my father, I thought he just knew.

Pictures of the Madonna and multiple prints of Padre Pio, the new beloved religious patriarch of Sicilians, adorn the walls. A large crucifix with a rosary coiled around it is above the headrest. The religion comes from *zia*. Uncle only believed in himself. Did *zia* know? A large green transport chest is at the foot of their wooden bed. An armoire, of the same dark veneer as the bed, and a porcelain washbasin on a stand complete this Spartan décor. His welcome had been so amiable, so hospitable, as if there had been no history, no past. As if no one had done anything wrong.

My skin crawls and I am reluctant to touch anything in this room. As a child, this bedroom had always been forbidden territory. I resolve to sleep in my clothes, on top of the sheets, and to barely move. Susan, slightly inebriated, could not begin to understand what I was feeling, and taking this adventure in stride, goes to the washroom, brushes her teeth and changes into the summer pyjamas she brought with her. After a peck on the cheek, and a declaration of love, she promptly falls asleep.

I can't sleep, but dare not toss around too much. Immobile, I stare straight up at the cracks in the ceiling stucco. The shadows and the cobwebs are lit by a slight moon that shines in through a small back window. I close my eyes.

Couscous in oversized plates, the cemetery, people dressed in black, my father, dirt pathways, my uncle, grandfather Salvatore, the edge of the mountain. The Mediterranean, a coffin, the fig tree, Rosetta, the castle, Antonio, my mother, Charlie, Susan… each image comes and goes, but still I can't sleep, and open my eyes to watch the shadows against the wall. I close my eyes again, and everyone is eating and laughing except Charlie and me. One more plate, one more glass of wine, one more memory, one more contradiction. Lizards are crawling all over my mother's body, and I let them. My father is tied to the fig tree and the lizards are gnawing at his feet. The fragments of images, in their repetitions and in their rearrangement, conspire to keep me awake. My stomach tries to regurgitate both dinner and indigestible memories. I fight back and send everything down. I try counting to a thousand. When there, I count backward to zero. The exercise sharpens my mind and I go back to thinking about my mother and my uncle. It wasn't right. Maybe I might have said something to my father, maybe that I saw them kiss. I am not even sure that the memory is correct. And what if I did tell my father, now everything is my fault. Sure, so easy, blame the victim. Fuck them.

An hour later I am still miserable, and because of that still awake, except that my bladder is ready to burst and I need to find a bathroom.

Silently cursing everyone and everything, I stumble my way to the side door that takes me to the garage-kitchen that leads to the washroom. I find it easily; the bathroom, although modernized, is in the same place. The lamppost outside the garage window slats gives enough light to guide me towards the door. I don't even need to reach for the light-switch.

My hand is on the knob of the bathroom door before I realize from the sliver of light under the door that it is occupied.

It is locked; there is a pause, and then the words "*Che cazzo*" come through the door, and then, "I'll be out in a minute."

Embarrassed, I say nothing and debate going back to bed, but the need to urinate is too strong and it keeps me standing to the side of the door. There is a faint smell of sweet smoke coming from the washroom.

"Charlie, it's me. Are you going to be long? I have to pee badly."

He doesn't answer.

I wait, and wait, cross my legs and wait some more.

The door finally opens, and he walks out smiling, a devilish smile with a 'got-you' smirk.

He looks me in the eyes, waits for my reaction, and says nonchalantly, "*Vado a Trapani, vuoi venire?*"

Did I want to go to Trapani with him?

"No!"

He stares, and notices that I am fully clothed.

"You look ready to go. I have the Vespa outside, we'll be there in no time, I'll bring you back when you want."

He's still smiling, knowing that this is not funny and that he shouldn't do this to me. He raises one perfectly tweezed eyebrow, and continues to smile a half-ironic, half-prankish smile. Although it should be, this is not a joke.

He asks as if we are in the middle of the afternoon, looking for something to do to pass the time, but it isn't like that at all. This isn't an invite for a *passeggiata* to the *Piazza*. The plan is a midnight escapade, a sortie with a Sicilian cousin, whose thinness is being back-lit by a dangling bathroom light, and whose long, shoulder-length hair is now tied in a tight pony tail, framing cheeks that he has brushed with rouge and lips that he has tainted with bright red lipstick, and wearing a short black dress over fishnet stockings, and whose pointy, razor-sharp high heels make him look taller. It is a shocking and incongruous picture of my cousin Charlie in full drag, smiling at me, and offering me a toke from a half smoked joint.

Did I want to go to Trapani with him looking like that? I don't think so.

"*Allora*? The club I'm going to has a rock and roll DJ tonight, all American music, it will be fun."

I don't answer. I am actually quite grossed out. I know about transvestites, I have seen them in Toronto, around Jarvis, or outside El Convento Rico, or during Pride Week, but this is different. Other people are transvestites, other people are gay, but not family members. My chest tightens, my stomach hurts.

He pushes for me to go. "You'll like it, see a different Sicily."

My silence tells him that I am not going, and he sounds disappointed. "I understand cousin, it's okay, it's not everybody's thing."

He says it as if he had misjudged me and then adds apologetically, "But cousin, it's too bad…."

Charlie quietly makes his way towards the door, picks up a pair of large denim overalls and slips them over his dress, takes off his shoes and puts on a pair of runners.

No longer in drag, and looking like a car mechanic, he says, "For the town, you know, in case… So cousin, for sure it's no?"

"I've got to pee."

# SEVEN

KEYS IN HAND, Charlie is waiting for me when I come out of the bathroom, and he asks again.

Of course I think, "Yes, it's no." When I do open my mouth, I stumble and stop after the word 'yes', and not because I want to say *yes* but because I want one more second to ask myself if there is any chance that I might want to go and do something different, something out of the ordinary, something to make me forget. I take too long to complete my answer, and let Charlie make the decision for me.

"*Sì. Bene. Allora andiamo. Sì.*"

And to convince myself that it isn't a mistake, that it is I who am in control, that it is *my* decision, I act as if I am more sure than I have ever been about anything, and I say with great confidence, "*Sì aspetta.* Let me tell Susan."

I go back to uncle's bedroom, shake and gently wake a very sleepy Susan and whisper, "I am going to Trapani with Charlie, do you want to come?" Knowing quite well that there is no room for three on a Vespa. And maybe I hope that she would wake up and stop me from doing this.

Susan only half opens her eyes, "No, no, you go, have fun. Apologize to Charlie for me. I'm too tired. Drank too much. Love you."

She is back asleep before I have time to kiss her goodnight.

☙

Charlie take's the northern route, the shorter, treacherous one, the one that zig-zags down the mountain and gets you to Trapani in twenty minutes. The one uncle and Rosetta took many years ago, to look for me. Charlie hasn't said a word, and neither have I, not that we can have much of a conversation. I had forgotten how precarious a Vespa ride can be. Being slapped by a stinging breeze, holding on to him while he negotiates this most dangerous highway is not the right time to discuss cross-dressing, or cross-gendering, or whatever sexual ambiguity he is into. My thoughts are more situational, more about how stupid of me it is to be riding on the back of a scooter without a helmet, with someone who has just finished smoking a joint, and also, more about my bad judgment for barrelling down such a dark and treacherous hill; and to make it worse, throughout the bumpy ride I keep thinking how strange it is that the perfume he is wearing is a Dolce & Gabbana scent I once gave to Susan as a birthday present, and which she liked very much. Worse than the fear that I might plunge over the hill and die is my inability to get rid of that feeling of disgust and anxiety I experienced at seeing Charlie in drag and in full makeup. And yet I can't deny the excitement of having been included in this adventure. The feeling is not unlike the one I had at the cemetery.

The ride doesn't take very long.

We motor through via Poeta Calvino, which I recognize from my childhood and which is off the main road that parallels the waterway. Here, I can smell the fish and the algae of the night-sea nearby. The 150cc engine roars, twists, and bounces along cobble-stoned streets that lead away from the port, and I hold on tightly. Not two minutes later, Charlie abruptly makes a sharp right at via Gatti, and stops in front of a long one-storey building made of dark wood and white stucco, called *'La barca'*. The club leans against the outer walls of the old town of Trapani, outside the ninth gate.

The Siculian Botanical Garden and via Garibaldi separate the building from the port's entrance, where the ferries to Tunisia are docked, and where earlier in the day we had seen the Arab and his camel.

Charlie dismounts right in front of the gated street, points to the corner of an iron-wrought balcony to the left of the old portal and says, "Cousin, look at that." I see part of a marble statue, which does not mean anything to me. "That head, did you know that it is put there to remind people of the story of *Don Serisso,* you know it?

"No."

"Well, this gate, Porta Serisso, is also named for him. The man butchered his unfaithful wife who was having an affair with their Tunisian servant, and he impaled her head on a broomstick, displaying it on the balcony as a warning to other Trapanese women to behave."

The barbaric act sends shivers down my spine. The shudders are quickly replaced by a sicker image of my mother's head on that balcony, as a beheaded adulteress.

*La barca* is well protected.

Facing us, backed in, front wheels erect and to the side, a motorcycle lineup provides a first line of defence against unwanted guests. The colourful and ubiquitous Vespas are to the right of the brightly lit entrance, while the thicker Japanese scooters, in semi-darkness and as if in disdain, are assigned the parking spots farthest away from the door. The big boys, Harleys, Hondas and BMW's, are to the left in descending order of size. Their left-leaning front wheels touch each other and make it impossible to squeeze between them from where we are.

Behind this iron levy, a few people are leaning against the wall. Others, forming small groups and out for a cigarette, are waving their arms and shaking their heads in loud agreements and even louder disagreements, blowing smoke and gesticulating in their own particular way, communicating more with their hands and body than with words.

I stand to the side waiting for Charlie to lift the Vespa up and backward onto its kickstand, positioning the scooter where a space had been left, it seems, just for him. He pulls down on the body-long zipper and slips out of his overalls. He rolls them up, and lifts the Vespa's seat that doubles as the lid for a small trunk. He shoves his outer clothes inside, pats himself down, adjusts his hair, freshens up his lipstick, and transforms himself into a beautiful woman. He delicately motions me to follow him, and I acquiesce.

The entrance to the club, a narrow path of flagstones between the lane of bikes, is blocked by clusters of sleeveless, muscular men, by women who maybe are and maybe are not women, and by men who definitely are not women, even though they are dressed like ladies of the night. Everyone seems way too happy.

I am apprehensive about disturbing this colourful insularity and step gingerly behind Charlie, but as if we had celebrity status, as they hear Charlie's voice and his greeting of *ciao ragazzi*, they smile, part, and let us through.

On the other side of this motorcycle moat, their backs to the building and to us, farther away, nearer to the Japanese scooters, another cluster of men, and of men in drag, stand leaning against the wall with an exaggerated sense of belonging. In that group, a tall emaciated twenty-something with a pink shirt opened wide and tied in a knot at the belt, a leg up and a knee out, looking like a beautiful one-legged flamingo, spots Charlie. The pink man-flamingo puts his foot down, interrupts his friends, and wildly motions towards us. The whole gaggle, as one, detaches itself from the wall. Charlie sees them and beams; they are the ones he was looking for. Their excitement builds as they bound forward, emitting little effeminate yelps from mostly ruby red lips. They warmly swarm my cousin. They hug and kiss Charlie as if he was a prodigal son, squeezing and holding his hands, genuinely happy to see him. I stand a bit to the side. Confused, fascinated, and slightly disgusted. I wait to be introduced.

After what seems like forever, they notice that I am standing there and throw inquiring looks towards my direction.

"*Amici*, how rude of me. He's my cousin, Salvatore. He's okay. Don't worry, I trust him. He's family, but in a good way." Charlie winks at me.

The pink shirt ignores me, turns back to Charlie and says in an exaggerated high pitched voice, "We didn't think you were coming. Ciccio said you had family stuff." He wipes the lipstick mark off Charlie's cheek with the inside of his thumb. His body is one twitching perpetual motion.

It takes me a moment to realize that I am the family stuff.

"When have I ever missed an *americanata* at *La barca,*" Charlie answers. "My cousin he's American, from Canada. He's straight, but *per favore amici*, make him feel at home."

Is that what all the *texting* had been about? He quickly introduces me to his friends.

"This is Chiara, Billy, Peppino, and Gulia. And of course, Ciccio, who you know from the bar."

In my nervousness, except for Ciccio, I forget their names as soon as he utters them. It may also be that although the women in the group are his friends, they are still guys in drag, and the guys in men's clothes are guys wearing what looks more like costumes, and the whole thing is surreal, and in the middle of Sicily, quite absurd and unimaginably stupid, and I can't look them in the face, and all I can think of is that I badly need a drink or two.

I politely and finally say, "*Ciao,*" and "*Buona sera,*" and I must look as uncomfortable and as silly as I feel.

Ciccio, perhaps sensing my discomfort, comes over and gives me a hug, two pecks on the cheek, and whispers in Petran, "Welcome to Charlie's world. Don't let it bother you."

I appreciate his friendliness.

"*Ragazzi, andiamo si fa tardi,*" says Billy, the pink shirt, gesticulating out of control, and we all follow his gait towards the entrance.

ঌ

Inside the club, a long rectangular room is badly lit by flickering votive candles in red glass containers. Garlands of multicoloured Christmas lights are strung on monolithic, blaring speakers that stand to each side of a small raised platform. There the DJ, slender body, sweating, shaved head, oversized headphones dangling from one ear, is lit by alternating yellows and reds, as a slow disco ball hovers above him. The small dance floor is half-full. The place has a run-down, hybrid Sixties-Seventies circa Roman Galley appearance. It is an old restaurant transformed into the bowels of a ship, with wooden paneling crisscrossed by shiny copper and bronze strips held together by large rivets. Faux-portholes are stuck against darkened windows. Thick and ancient four by six beams hold up a ceiling made of cheap knotty planks. Empty rum barrels and other naval sundries are strewn haphazardly throughout the room, while Toulouse-Lautrec prints of gay Paris and posters of the American navy adorn the walls, a mish-mash of styles as odd as the clientele.

At the bar, Charlie and his friends order brightly coloured martinis, except for Ciccio, who has red wine, and I who ask for a double shot of vodka with no ice. I try paying for their drinks, which they at first refuse, and then remembering the old Sicilian adage of asking three times, I insist three times and they accept. I tell them in my fractured Sicilian that I am happy to meet them and to be here, although I admit to them that I find this place an unusual setting, one I am not used to, one that makes me anxious, and I laugh. They appreciate my honesty, and my generosity. Well coiffed heads nod and smile. I can't say that I feel at home but I do feel better after draining that first drink.

"*È carino tuo cugino*," says Chiara, who is a guy. She gets closer, and is ready to flirt with me although she was told not to. The group rolls their eyes as if to say here she goes again.

Her attention is a compliment I would have accepted from any woman, but not from one who looks like a woman but is definitely too masculine to be one. The boa and the effete mannerisms do not fool me, and so I thank her, adding that I am straight and married. Charlie is the only one who can truly pass as a woman in this place. As a woman, Charlie has changed; he's no longer a timid, vulnerable young man; he looks secure and confident. Gulia, I hate to think it because she is so nice and always smiling, is one ugly woman. She should have stayed a guy. The other men/women have such tight dresses that I wonder where they hide their balls, and that also is a thought I didn't think I would ever have.

"*Grazie*," I say shyly to Gulia, but making sure that I am not perceived as flirting back.

I order another double shot of vodka, while everyone else is still on their first drink.

The flapping pink shirt looks and me and laughs; but not in a kind way, more like mocking me. I don't think he likes me; he's Sicilian suspicious.

The song, *It's my party and I'll cry if I want to*, comes on. The dance floor quickly fills up with hips swinging, mouths lip-synching, and hands moving. As my eyes get used to the darkness, I see more naval paraphernalia, centuries of seafaring knick-knacks, wooden treasure chests, periscopes, and even one large rusty anchor. An oversized helm is suspended from the ceiling.

With the song over, my new friends return to the bar.

I assume that there will be a drag show, which would account for some of the clothes/costumes that people are wearing. I ask Ciccio, who is staying close to me. Unlike them he is dressed in jeans and polo shirt. He answers my query by saying that the real show is on the dance floor, and then laughs before saying "no" there won't be any *entertainment*.

Small bottles of bubble soap appear on the tables and Charlie begins playing with one of them. Blowing into a small plastic loop, he releases tiny bubbles that the light from the disco-ball infuses with sparkles. He aims the bubbles at his friends, who try to catch them between their fingers or on their tongues. One adventurous couple attempts to snare a large, slow floating bubble between their puckered lips. I'm actually feeling a bit better, less grossed out. The pink flamingo and the other dancers are swaying to old rock and roll. Unlike me, they all seem at ease, having unadulterated fun, almost innocent in a cocooned world sort of way.

Chiara taps her foot and then asks me to dance. I politely refuse; giggling and winking, she says that she understands.

I order another glass of wine for Ciccio and a shot of vodka for me, since we're the only two from our group not dancing.

"Ciccio, you… Are you," I motion with my head, "like them?"

"No, Sacred Saints, no, are you crazy, I love women. I am here because I like the music, and Charlie is my good friend, I look after him, watch his back. No, I have a girlfriend, she lives in Palermo. We are going to get married next year."

"Congratulations… And live in Petra?"

"No, and that's another problem. As soon as I can, I'll have to tell my parents that I don't want to run the bar anymore, that I am leaving, for good. They'll go nuts on me. The bar has been in our family for generations."

"You've got to do what you have to do."

A stupid cliché that sounds even lamer in this place.

"That's for sure, but Palermo is not far and we will visit. Family is important."

We stop talking and go back to looking at the dance floor. The spinning disco ball bathes the dancers in the yellows, reds and whites of gleaming teardrops.

"Tell me, Ciccio, do they really want to be women? Because I have to tell you some are not that pretty as women. Or are they playing, like being at a costume party?"

He laughs and agrees with me that they are not all pretty. We get catty and rate the men/women one to ten, with Charlie being a ten.

"About what you were saying. I don't know much. Some are transvestites, you know, just clothes, some are gay and like to play dress-up, have fun, some are like Charlie and do it for business, well, then there are also a few who say that they are women in a man's body; they also do it for business. But, they want the operation."

"That's pretty fucked. What do you mean *business*?"

He makes a look that shows he doesn't understand that I don't understand.

The music gets louder and I'm having a problem hearing him describing the different people he knows in here, and I give up. I don't quite see the differences between these people; they all appear to be the same, men with too much makeup dressed as women dancing with men with less makeup but no less effeminate.

The cacophony of sounds and motion along with the drinking is relaxing me and I tap on the bar counter. Everyone is dancing; they've even enticed Ciccio. Charlie invites me to join their group dance, but not being drunk enough I thank him and stay at the bar. They're funny. They do a strange type of modern line dancing to an old American tune I don't remember. They all know the moves and they are having fun in their synchronicity of leg kicking, jumping, stomping, turning on the spot to the right, to the left, arms swinging rhythmically.

I finish my drink and order another one. The vodka is harsh on the throat, but I am beginning to enjoy the alcohol and the heat it brings with it. I also feel much better about being here, better able to appreciate their innocence, but not better enough to dance with guys. I feel less like a stranger or an impostor.

"I'll be right back, stay with Ciccio."

Charlie and most of the gang disappear, go outside.

"Ciccio, where did they go?"

"You know, here and there. They go and make their money."

"Make money?"

"You really don't know what's going on?"

I actually don't know. Ciccio closes his hand into a loose fist and brings it up repeatedly towards his mouth, making sucking sounds while puffing-up his cheek. He laughs, and then presses his thumb against his index finger and slides it up and down; the universal sign for money.

"It's disgusting… Charlie?"

"Him too!"

I want to throw up.

ଓ

Holding on to the bar, I get up from the stool. I let go. A mistake. Off-balance, I lean to one side and then to the other. I try to will the dizziness away, but it only stops when I grab onto the edge of the bar. I endeavour for no reason to walk towards the dance floor, to look for Charlie, to ask him to his face, to tell him to stop this disgusting thing he does. I can't get rid of Ciccio's sordid hand-gesture, and when I do, I think of my uncle and my mother and their sordidness, and I don't know which is worse. I try to walk, and the small steps are another sign that I am definitely intoxicated. I soon give up on walking and return to the comfort of my barstool.

"Water please."

I ask the bartender, but the words come out differently, I am slurring, and if I can tell, I know that he also can. The music is louder than I remembered it. I know the words of this song and search for a title. My mind doesn't help.

"Bottled water is fine. A tall one, *frizzante,* please."

The bottle is sweating, my hands are wet and I can't twist the top off.

"Wet and slippery, like my dick."

Billy laughs at his own dirty joke, but does not offer to help. Everything is louder, the voices, the laughter. Everything is brighter, the metallic eye shadow on men trying to be women, the vibrant women's clothes on men, and the long coarse wigs on the men's heads. Everything is spinning, the disco ball, the dancers, my head. Charlie, who has just come back, grabs the bottle from me and takes the top off with one forceful twist and hands it back.

"Are you okay?" He asks, knowing quite well that I am drunk.

"Yes, I'm fine."

But I'm not. I can't look him in the eyes, or look at his scarlet lips, nor can I look at any of his friends. I'm disgusted.

Billy and Chiara's lips are moving but I can't make out the words. Sharing a joke? Laughing at me? They should look at themselves. I am annoyed at myself for not seeing my drunkenness coming. I also don't care, which is another sign that I have had too much to drink. The girls are looking at me, I mean the boys. And so, they're all prostitutes, even ugly Giulia? Men dressed as women giving blowjobs. Pretty fucking disgusting. One long gulp of cold water and the bubbles tickle the back of my throat. The sound of my Adam's apple going up and down is amplified and I stop only when the bottle is half empty.

"Are you okay?" Charlie asks again.

"Fine. I'm fine!!"

"You seem angry, did something happen?"

"No!"

"You want to go home?"

"No!"

"Are you sure?"

What am I to say? Stop sucking cocks. Am I supposed to stop him from earning his drug money? His clothes money, his fag money?

"Yes! I'm sure."

"Do you want to dance?"

"No! Nooooo!"

"Do you mind if I go?"

"No!"

Charlie joins Chiarra and Billy on the dance floor as soon as he hears the first note of an old American rock and roll song I can't place. I know this song too. Tip of my tongue. I try different titles and none of them fit. Chuck Berry sings it. This is a different band, but the song is the same. Charlie's backside, made womanlier by the short dress and the high heels, swings side to side. What am I doing here?

I've got to stop judging, I'm just a guest here. The alcohol is helping to tame my feelings of disgust. People are popping pills, chasing them down with Red Bull. Chiarra, and his friend, the pink man-flamingo, offer me a red pill and out of habit I refuse. I can't tell if it's ecstasy or speed, and since I don't know the Italian words for either, and since I'm not sure I want to go there, I politely decline his second offering. He says it's safe and to trust him. I say no again. I'll stick to water and try to sober up. The last thing I need is drugs.

"Okay cousin?"

I can't keep my mouth shut.

"Charlie."

"*Sì*?"

"Charlie, Ciccio told me about what you guys do. Is it true?"

I repeat Ciccio's crude gesture. Charlie takes a moment before answering.

"So, it bothers you?"

"Yes."

"I'm sorry it offends you. You want to leave?"

"Do you?"

"No! Do you?"

"I don't know."

"Look, cousin, if at any time you want to leave, just let me know, and with no hesitation I'll take you home."

"No...."

"I'm sorry, cousin, I thought you understood, that's how it is here. It's not like that in America? Men in dresses, that's what they do in Italy. Sorry. May I go?"

"Go."

He slowly walks away, and looks back to make sure that I am all right. I put up a front and smile; I give him the thumbs up. I soon lose him in the crowd.

Another song. Another one that I know, but unlike the others it is not an American song, it is the one that Charlie played in the car. The one with Arabic sounds.

"Ciccio, do you know this song?"

"Yes, it's by Farouk Brahmen, a Tunisian singer."

"Charlie likes that song."

"Yes, they are playing it for him. He likes Tunisian things. He has a friend in Tunis, one day he's going to join him, that's what he says. I know he'll never go."

"Have you met his friend?"

"No, he doesn't say much about him. It's a big secret."

Sitting is good. Standing is better. No, sitting is the right choice. The ledge of the bar is my friend. Look at them. A real fucking gay parade in here. People look at me. Me. They're the weirdos. I stare back. Looks like a float of Pride Day drag queens crashed *La barca*. I laugh.

"Sorry," I say in English.

This whole thing is fucking wrong. Cock-sucking queens as my friends and relatives is messed up. It's repulsive really. Unnatural. All the fucking pretending. Pirandello would have loved it. He could have written his heart out watching these guys. Like fishing in a barrel. Pretensions my ass, it's all about cock sucking and ejaculating. They want to be women. Good for them, they can have it. What for, and who are they kidding? In the dark, I can't even tell whose tits are real and whose are not; some look pretty good. But the makeup, way too much, don't they know, almost on purpose, I sure don't understand, and now I want another drink, and I better not. There were real women when we first came in. *Slow it down, Sal, drink water.* I do. Where are those real women? Booze always makes me horny, which is good, best memories, some of the worst too, which is why just water for me from now on. I drain the rest of the San Pellegrino and order vodka on the rocks.

"Premium?"

My new male-prostitute friends keep popping pills.

I can't believe my mother. What did she see in uncle? He was different from my father. So different is good? Did the whole town know? Did my father really not know?

The bartender looks at me funny. I don't know why. My Italian, my slurring, both. He serves me anyway and I give him a good tip. I'll keep the full glass on the counter, save it for later. Just water for now. Right. I smile, pick the vodka up and drain the shot in one gulp. Fuck the water, fuck the bartender, and fuck drunkenness. With an open hand full of pills, Billy offers a red capsule. I take it on the first offering; fuck Sicilian codes. I thank him and swallow it. He says that it will keep me awake. What about the purple one? Those are different. "For tripping," he says. He puts the rest away. I love the taste of alcohol when I am drunk. Wash down the pill. Vodka and a little red pill. Cold, hot. There are women who hang around gays and transvestites. There are some in this club, I know. What are they called? Gay whores, gay friends, gay hags, who the fuck remembers. Here just for the dancing. Gays find women safe to party with. I read that somewhere. For a good time. For an asexual good time, go with gay. Their loss. I'd give those women a *good* sexual time, a good fuck, that's for sure. I'd show those fags how to treat a beautiful woman. I need to get up and look for one. I'll fall if I get up, better not. Would these real women not get real horny watching these beautiful men, if they were straight, I mean? I am sure they would. Well I am here if they want me.

"Charlie, why? Do you need the money that badly?"

"Cousin it's not just about the money, it helps but…" He shrugs his shoulders, "It's complicated."

"Okay."

"It's hard to explain… I feel different as a woman, sexy, desired. I never feel that way as a guy."

"Okay."

*I feel sexy as a woman,* he's got to be kidding, he's sucking cocks for money.

He's fucked and delusional. They all are. What about me? I make good money without sucking cocks. Mind you I do kiss ass. That's funny. So I am a conservative bank manager. So I minimize risk, lend, make profits for head office, and wait for my Christmas bonus. What's wrong with that? Better than them. Look at those two on the dance floor, dry fucking. No penetration. Good foreplay. What next? Get a room, fagots. I can't understand this whole thing about dressing up as a woman and making out with a gay guy. They're both guys, right? And why does one have to play the male role and one the female role, when they are both men with cocks? I can't resist any longer. One more drink, just one. Down the throat it goes. The alcohol is cold and harsh. It feels good. Less unsteady. Gays have the right idea; just fuck anything on two legs. Makes them the perfect whores. Wouldn't fucking all the time get boring?

"*Acqua minerale, per favore… Frizzante.*"

Too loud; the bartender gives me another one of his looks. He hates me, I am a stranger, they hate strangers in Sicily, I should tell him that I was born here, I am still a foreigner, they hate foreigners. I love watching people dance. I stare ahead. Catatonic by choice. Happy in a strange way that I came. Charlie is not a bad guy, totally fucked, but not a bad guy. Susan is right about me getting worse; I am less interested in life. As I get older I become more like my father, a little less communicative, a little less engaged. How far can I push before she leaves me?

"Sometimes, cousin, it's simply about feeling wanted, and as a woman I'm always wanted."

"Bullshit."

"I see it in their eyes, in their smiles, they get excited, and I am the one that's creating the excitement. And *that* also excites me."

"Bullshit."

"I'm desired."

Bullshit, his sucking lips are what are desired.

"It makes me feel good."

"*These boots are made for walking*" comes on, Nancy Sinatra's, and I like this song. My mind wanders away from Charlie and back to my parents.

My mother was unhappy. My father was unhappy. My uncle made my mother happy, and then my father took her away, and she became unhappy again. It was so simple. Oh yes, in all their happiness and unhappiness, they also forgot about me. She misunderstood me, I didn't hate her because of her affair, that was my excuse, I hated her because she never held me close, because she never told me that she loved me. Even admitting that she didn't want me, that I was a mistake, would have been better. I wouldn't have kept waiting and hoping.

"*And these boots will walk all over you....*"

# EIGHT

SHE'S STARING. THE short red dress, the curves, the lips, the full breasts, and I am excited because I finally see a woman who has a real cleavage; and as quickly as that, I'm not, because I could be wrong; but then I think, I am not so drunk that I can't tell a real woman when I see one.

A moot point anyway, because it is too late, I'm too drunk and I'm no longer interested. Charlie has left me alone. I don't want to meet anyone, or to talk to anyone. I just want to sit at the bar. I'm not a happy drunk. When I get drunk, I hate everyone. I'm proud of the way I hate; the drinking gives me license to detest as much as I want. I go internal and silently say things like, I hate you and you and you, I hate the rain, the night, and you the man with the baseball hat, and you the girl with the stupid blue shoes. In my imagination I point fingers. Tonight, I imagine saying things like I hate men who pretend to be women, I hate small towns like Petra and people who live in them, I hate Sicily, I hate my uncle, I hate my mother; and my father, who is more to be pitied than hated, I also hate. And most definitely and most vociferously, I can say that I hate what I have become.

She's still staring.

*She*, for sure, is a woman, but I am no fool and I don't want there to be a cock between her thighs, and so I stare back. I look at her shapely legs, at her body and everything that is woman is in all the right places, and I focus on her black fishnet stockings, trying to avoid her face and her own stare, unwittingly getting excited. I look down at her ankles, at a thin gold bracelet, at her absurdly long and pointy pumps, and say nothing.

"*Ti piace?*" She says, in a sweet, slow, dramatic, open-mouth voice, but in a voice that is wrong, a woman's vocal cords transformed by what might have been a nasty cold, by smoke damage, or a voice raspy from swollen glands, or even a strangely peculiar voice one was cursed with at birth.

I try more excuses, but I doubt each and every one of them, not in this place. But I don't want to ask and I don't want to ogle; yet I need to know, so I furtively catch a glimpse. Her skin is smooth, and blemish free, her nose is uncharacteristically long and straight, perfect in every way and without any tell-tale signs of a cold. I turn away when she catches me having stared.

As if needing more proof, I hurriedly peek at her breasts while she looks away towards the dance floor, and I don't see any signs of a bra either but of breasts shaped like black Asian pears that show a hint of a nipple under a slim, and low-cut, tight dress.

She turns back to me.

"*E che fai qui?*"

Her voice is sweet, melodic and so low that it throws me off. I stutter.

"I'm here with… My cousin, but I am… Not…" I don't know the Italian word for gay or drag queen or transvestite or even straight. Stumbling over the language, unable to answer properly, and a bit too loudly, I let out the word "*Omo… Omosessuale,*" and continue to search for her sexuality. It is stupid of me to have said that, and I should say something to show that I am not that stupid, and that I'm simply confused and drunk. She nods and her long lashes uncover very dark irises centring very white and very bright eyes. She catches me looking at her thick pink eye shadow and answers my stare with a perfect, wide smile. She's a striking, tall, thin black woman in a short dress casually leaning against the bar. I look away. I have never befriended black women before. I don't know why, and maybe I have been a bit afraid of them. But this woman is different, mysterious, yet warm and welcoming. She comes closer, I like her smell, it's an out-of-the-shower fresh scent, and although apprehensive, I am beginning to like that she's paying attention to me.

I continue to avoid her eyes, and pretend to look behind her, but I surreptitiously glance.

"*Ti piace guardare.*"

The low voice, à la Turner, is quite sexy, except that it is too low.

"Sorry, I didn't mean to stare. You are very beautiful."

It just came out, and it was the wrong thing to say. I am still not sure that she's not a he, and I should not be encouraging her.

"*Grazie, lo so sei il cugino di Charlie.*"

Did she mean she knew she was beautiful or that she knew that Charlie was my cousin? She's confusing me. Her voice keeps betraying her body, and her face betraying her voice. She is coming on to me, and I like that, elegantly dressed and no sign of a bulge between her legs. She knows who I am, and she knows I am straight and yet she keeps smiling. She bats her eyelashes and moves her hands in a way that is ever so slightly too feminine.

"*Sì*," I answer her.

"*Sei carino!*"

She says that I am cute, and I allow those alluring words to repeat in my head, so as to make sure that I fully understand them, and that there is no doubt about the flirting. She puts her hands together and brings them to her heart. A sweet, and very girly, gesture. But her voice is lower than mine, and though not completely a turnoff, it makes me wonder, makes me want to ask. I decide that if she had wanted to fool me she would have disguised her voice and therefore she must be a woman.

I turn away from her and look at the dance floor; the couple from earlier are back at it, dry humping in front of us. Embarrassing really. This thin, gorgeous black woman beside me smiles, and laughs when she sees what I am looking at, and I think I may be giving her the wrong impression, so I look at the posters of the US Marines on the walls, and that also may be giving her the wrong impression.

"My name is Simone, but people call me '*La Marocchina*'. Can I buy you a drink?" She says in a perfect Italian man's voice coming from a pair of beautiful, deeply grooved, and deeply purpled, black woman's lips.

I say again that I'm here with my cousin, visiting.

"Yes, I know. Everyone knows Charlie, and I know him more." She winks and laughs.

My drunken thoughts get tongue-tied, and I have to stop drinking, if only for a little while, so that I can think better.

"*Acqua, per favore.*"

Simone tells me that she is Ethiopian, which explains the Italian.

"Ethiopia is not a good place," she says.

I feel sorry for her, and at another time, somewhere else, in a language I can better express myself in, I would have loved to have a conversation.

I keep looking at her, trying to figure it out, part of me wanting her to be a woman, part of me not caring.

Like Charlie, she walks on what must be excruciatingly painful stiletto heels.

She takes the stool to my left, turns towards me, and exposes her fishnetted thighs, folding one leg over the other. I peek at the darkness between her legs and I feel a twinge between my own legs. Old habit. I wonder if she had a sex change and then I banish the thought and look at her beautiful breasts instead, breasts I would very much like to touch.

She flatters me, and even with her deep voice, it feels good to have someone so beautiful flirting with me, paying attention to me. If I can continue to balance the vodka with the San Pellegrino water, I'll be fine. A song by Little Richard comes on, and the dance floor is doing the twist. I bob my head up and down to the music and so does Simone. I remember that she asked a question and I answer her, giving me another opportunity to linger on her smooth and glittering dark face, to search for gender.

"No, thanks, I am already too drunk." I smile, and she playfully grins.

She orders champagne for herself and vodka for me.

"You shouldn't have. I can't. . . ."

She comes closer, lifts the flute of champagne to her lips, "*Salute*," sips it, puts it down gently, touches my elbow and asks.

"A dance? *Vuoi ballare*?"

She is not listening to me. I am flattered though, and she is sweet, but I need to let this, whatever this is, go, and besides I am awful on the dance floor, and besides that, what does she not understand about the fact that I am not gay; or more importantly what message am I sending her, and what is it that *I* don't understand.

"No, I am not...."

I want to make sure that she understands that I am not like the others here, that I am a visitor, a guest, a voyeur at most, but that I am straight. I struggle again with words I am unfamiliar with, and keep saying that I am a *man*, *uomo*, but when I think that she finally understands me, she says in her own man's voice, "I know. *Vieni*," and softly grabs my hand.

She is gentle and I let her; it is easier than to argue. Too tired to argue. Too drunk to argue. The touch, the hold, the softness, the tightness, the being led, the black thing, the being led thing, the losing control thing, it all feels good, it all feels right... Which is undeniably the most stupid thought I have ever had. No, the second most stupid because the first is that I am holding her hand, and... And, I'm not repulsed. Simone carves a path and guides me to the dance floor. People move for her, they know of her; I'm her dance partner and, as incongruous as it seems, I accept that fact and let her lead me. Stupidly, it even makes me feel important. She could have anyone but she chose me. Without having asked her if she's a man or a woman I let her take me to the dance floor. In the middle, cosseted by sweating scented bodies, I sway to the music and to my alcoholism. Here everything is less wrong. She sustains me. She anchors me as the bar stool had done earlier. The air is thick with flashing greens and reds from the overhanging, slow-turning disco-ball, turning even slower while my head spins. Her sweet scent comes in waves, as she moves closer and backs away, as she lightly bumps me and moves back. The wiry and quirky DJ changes the pace, slows it down with a jazzy tune, infused with Arabic and Middle Eastern beats. I think that we should go back, because it is not an appropriate dancing song.

"No," I say to her.

"No?" she says to me.

We stay on the dance floor.

"I know that music," I tell her.

"It's Farouk Brahmen," she tells me.

It's neither fast nor slow. Couple's choice, it could be either. Most couples go for slow. I am not that drunk. I know what's going on here. I go for fast. Her arms come around me. Clasp me. She wants a slow dance. She says that I am hers for the night. She laughs. It's just for fun. Maybe the dizziness will go away, if I hold on tight. I go along. I do my one-two steps in place, without moving much. The disco ball lights us and I close my eyes.

"Sorry. I am such a bad dancer," I apologize.

The acids in my stomach come up half way and for the second time tonight, with great effort I manage to push them back and not throw up on this person who calls herself *La Marocchina* and who likes me, and who has me dancing with her. But I must leave space between us, just hands touching; that's okay, right? I move back, stumble, start again.

"Sorry," I apologize.

I trip over her feet. She grabs me before I fall and holds me closer than before. Touch is touch and close is close. I am okay with it, I need someone to hold me or I'll fall, it might as well be her, there is no one else to hold on to, and I relax. Simone smiles. She wraps her arms tightly around my shoulders and leans her head against mine. She smells good; a fresh citric sent. Her thigh brushes against mine, she leaves it there, dancing against it, and I feel myself getting aroused and I move away. This is just dancing I tell myself. I can explain. No, I can't. I tighten up again at the thought of my wife seeing me like this. Of anyone seeing us. I feel nothing; it's not sexual. Which is good, which is normal, right? Simone gently caresses me. The soft of her fingers against the back of my neck relaxes me. This woman who I barely know, knows what I like. She knows what I need. It's not sexual; it's like the night I danced with Paul, when we were both drunk. It's like getting a massage from a man masseur. Her bright straight red hair cascades down my back.

As she nudges deeper into my shoulder blade, I feel the almost imperceptible pursing of her lips gently kissing and wetting my neck, sending tiny shudders down my spine. Now this has to be wrong. It *is* sexual. And I see the big red stop sign. Her cheek is soft. This is way wrong, I'm married, *wrong because you're married, or wrong because she may be a guy*. I am scared and excited… It's still wrong. She tightens her hold on me and presses her thigh against mine, moving it to the inside, pushing it between my legs; each dance step, each beat, a short pelvic thrust, and a caress and a soft kiss. It feels good. She's good. She's sweet. I know she wants me. My body responds in kind. My eyes close. I sway. A thrust, a caress, a kiss, each one better than the last. Her scent stronger, her touches softer, she crawls inside me. I open my eyes, the lights around the DJ booth are a brighter red, the disco-ball is bathing us in white light, and Chiara and Billy are dancing nearby. They look at me, say something that I don't hear. Billy extends his hand, asks with his head, and as I nod he puts the purple pill in my mouth. Chiara laughs. Simone brings me back to her. I am the people I was looking at earlier and making fun of. I don't care. I smile. Simone ignores the other dancers, draws me away, and continues to lean into me. Her kissing lips, the rippled moistness of figs, are wet traces that slowly make their way to my ear lobes and delicately embrace them, gobbling them, penetrating them. Breathing into my ears, her tongue unfurls, licking with warm upward strokes and slow, downward kisses that make me tremble.

"*Ti piace.*"

Asking me if I like it or if I like her is not fair.

The thrusting becomes deeper and faster, moving to Farouk's intensifying jazz beat. My eyes close again. In darkness, all is better. Her lips find mine. Her tongue finds mine. I suck on her tongue and that feels good. I small-bite her thick African lips. I become hard, and as she opens up her legs a bit wider for me, I can also feel her erection rubbing against mine. She doesn't have a cunt. And it should be bad and it is not bad because it feels good. I dare not open my eyes; I dare not know where I am. Simone bites back and her strong white teeth draw a hint of blood, a hint of saltiness, a hint of sweat, a hint of hot desert, harder and harder, our teeth knock against each other, her serpentine tongue draws my insides into her. I hold on tighter and stop moving. Mollified by alcohol, my body moulds itself into her sexuality. She kisses me again, again and again, small kisses, all over the face, the neck, the cheeks, and she grabs my face with her two hands and her wide tongue is back into my mouth, and since I can't resist anymore, I let myself go, and I ejaculate against her red dress, again and again. One last thrust, one last explosion and a cold shiver runs down my spine. She holds on to my tightness and absorbs me into her thighs, her whole body, a vigorous embrace that ties me to her, and in her I can feel the calmness, the breeze and the slight wetness of a dreamy oasis when suddenly she begins to shake and quiver, and I can't help but return the kindness and take her into me.

The song ends, she quickly grabs my hand and says, "Come with me, *bello*."

☙

Outside of *La barca*, it feels different; she pushes me against the wall. Unbuckles me. Puts her hand down my pants. Pulls and jerks on a wet penis that now refuses to get hard. Her gentleness is gone. The nails dig hard. It hurts and I tell her to stop. She stops. Tries to kiss me. I turn my head. She lands on my cheek, settles for love bites all along my neck, but it's not sexy anymore. What she wanted was no longer what I wanted.

"Wait, hold on," she slides down along my body, her mouth looking for my cock. It's not exciting anymore. It's disgusting.

"No." I push her away.

"*Dai lascia*."

"No. Please leave me alone. Where is my cousin?"

"Forget about Charlie, let me, you'll like it. I'm the best."

She's no longer sweet, she's vulgar, and her low voice adds to the harshness of her words. It reminds me of my uncle's vulgarities.

"NO!"

She pulls herself up and tries to kiss me again, but I pull away. I fall backward on tangled bodies, and one of them angrily yells, "*Vaffanculo*."

I answer in kind by telling them to go fuck themselves, and add that they probably already did, which makes me laugh. The larger of the two shadows comes at me, having understood more English than I thought, wanting to strike me, but Simone gets in front. I keep laughing and taunt the queers to go find a hotel.

Simone explains to the men that I am drunk, and apologizes for me, says that I am with her, and not to mind me, that I am confused. She grabs my hand and drags me further away. She holds, caresses, and pulls me across the street, towards the Botanical Gardens.

I want to find Charlie. I want to think clearly. I want to be sober. I need her to stop and let me go. I want everything to stop spinning. I want everyone to leave me alone.

"I am not *Omosessuale*. I am not like Charlie."

She ignores my words, and assists me over a low chain that fences the entrance to the Gardens. A lit path, with wooden benches, winds itself around the trees.

I call for Charlie while trying to walk away from her.

"Where are you going?" she squeals.

Her sexy voice now irritates me.

Taking drunken small steps, I sway from one side to the other side of the dirt path. I am stumbling. I'm searching for Charlie. I have to find Charlie. I say it in English and I say it loudly in Italian. I want Charlie to take me home, I have had enough of these people, and I scream for him.

"*Sei uno stupido*, we're not finished," Simone says sweetly, following me, a few paces behind.

I run between trees and momentarily lose her. There are shadows and quiet conversations all around. I'm scared. My eyes adjust to the darkness of this wooded lot and an older man in a suit-jacket, with a jovial round face, is standing, leaning against the back of a bench, looking away from me. In front of him, a kneeling shadow of someone dressed as a woman has her head buried in his crotch. I see where they make their money. The standing man turns towards me; I catch his face in the light of a lamppost and with a hint of self-satisfaction, he smiles.

I yell, "CHARLIE!"

# NINE

THE MAN IN drag looks up, and to my relief she is not my cousin.

"Charlie!" I continue calling, trying to find him in the darkness.

Simone reappears and shoves me against a tree.

Exhausted, tired of running, I close my eyes to the feel of her crotch against my crotch, to her breasts against my chest, to her red wig sweeping against my cheek, to her scent that overpowers me once more, and to her hands slithering, unbuttoning the clasp of a belt I had just buckled, unzipping a zipper I had just pulled up. I open my eyes to a violent dizziness, ready to throw up all over her red dress, and to stop myself I scream in my loudest Sicilian.

"*Vattene! Non ti voglio!*"

Deaf to my telling her to go away, to my saying that I don't want her, she keeps pushing against me, and I keep rejecting her.

"No!"

Inches from her face, I shout for her to stop, push her off, and for the second time tonight I pull my pants up, and maybe because the fighting has made me less drunk, less numb, I can feel my grandfather's clasped knife scraping against my leg, and I remember that I have a weapon.

"Simone. I told you to stop."

She won't. I retrieve *nonno's* heirloom, and with a quick flip of the wrist the blade flickers.

"*Finiscila... Figlia di buttana,*" I yell.

Simone stops at the word, *buttana,* surprised at the harshness of the Petran word for whore. She sees my knife and laughs, says words like ludicrous, ignorant, and comes back at me, extending her hand towards my crotch, as if she was certain that I would never do anything so stupid as to stab her. She slips her hand between my legs, squeezes gently, and I forcefully slap her arm away. The roughness stuns her, and once again she momentarily retreats.

"I swear I'll cut you if you don't stop."

"*No carino*! You're not capable," she says, mocking my attempts at scaring her off, laughing in my face, following me further inside the park where the trees have disappeared behind the fog.

"You don't know me," I tell her.

"*Sì ti conosco; sei come gli altri.*"

And in her perfect Italian that she learned in Ethiopia, she tells me that she knows me, that I am a man and therefore like the others. Abruptly, she lunges, snares my wrist and puts the steel blade against her own neck, tempting me to puncture her.

"*Uccidimi*, kill me, go ahead...."

I try to pull the knife away from her throat, but, weakened by alcohol and fatigue, I'm easily pinned against the trunk.

Gripping my hand, and using her body to hold me there, she presses the knife into her own skin and shows me how she's not afraid of me or of a small cut; that she's had her share. On the contrary, as if turned-on by the possibility of pain, and as the tip of the blade pricks her dark skin, drawing small beads of blood, she rubs my crotch with her knee. Panting and excited, she gives me a let-me-or-kill-me ultimatum, and tries kissing me, while holding my wrist and the knife to her neck.

"You're crazy."

"Some people pay extra to see blood," she says.

"Fuck you, Simone!"

Again the meanness of those English words that she knows too well shocks her, and momentarily she weakens her grip. Taking full advantage of her surprise, I pull the knife away from her neck, push her off, and step away from the tree, making quick left-to-right slashes with the blade.

"Don't come near me again."

It has the opposite effect, she comes closer, jousting with me, skipping from side-to-side, moving forward and backward, playing a dangerous game, barely avoiding the sharp thrusts.

"You can't," she laughs.

I hear my voice say, "I'm finished talking to you."

"What you're gonna do? You're just a mama's boy with a limp cock. Let me help you."

I hear myself scream one last warning, which she also ignores, and then I let my grandfather's knife, with one steady swipe to the left, slice through her red dress. And on the return jab, I angrily burrow the knife deeper and rip the skin along her midriff, opening a razor-thin but body-wide incision.

"*Sei un vero stronzo*. You think I'm scared of a small cut."

The blood begins to ooze from the fraying edges of the dress, exposing a flesh now streaked with blotching red marks. My hand doesn't stop there, and firmly stuck to the handle, it pushes the knife inward and twists.

Simone looks down at her gash, at my hand, and then at my sullen face, smirks as if saying, "Look what you have done you silly boy," as if she is only worried that I have ruined her new dress, as if there is no pain from the nasty cut.

"Go on, continue," she dares.

The blade of its own accord wraps itself around the folds of her open stomach, grafting a bloodied dress to chunks of loose skin, and continues its evisceration, but Simone is not feeling any of it; instead she keeps laughing at me.

ଔ

"Cousin, *che cazzo fai*?"

I have never been so glad to hear such a familiar voice.

"Charlie…"

"Ciao, Simone."

"Ciao, Charlie."

Simone's mischievous eyes are locked on mine while she greets Charlie. The blade inside of her is in deeper than before and the old ivory handle, now covered in blood, is barely visible.

"Charlie help me."

He sits on the park bench across from where we are standing, stares at us and shakes his head.

"What do you want me to do, cousin? You're really gone."

"I know, but don't just sit there Charlie, come here, do something."

He must not be seeing how Simone's dress unravels along the sharp edge of the slicing blade, bloodies, and bunches-up above her hips, showing a short white girdle and the outline of a man's crotch that also quickly becomes drenched in its own dark blood.

"Here, have another orange," he says, as if this was nothing.

I unwittingly sever a layer of longitudinal muscles and they snap back, making the abrasion around her stomach worse. The cavity surrounding her dangling belly button gets wider, sucking my fingers in up to their knuckles, getting them wet and sticky, and for the second time tonight I am both disgusted and exhilarated.

"*Lasciala.* Just give her the money."

My cousin asks me to let her go, but he doesn't understand that at this moment my hand is not my own, and that everything I do is involuntary and that instead of hurting Simone, I'm simply knifing her into a greater, frenzied shaking. The larger the incision the more orgiastic she becomes. She screams her pleasure and wheezes in delight with each thrust.

"Charlie, do you see how she reacts?"

"Cousin, where did you get the knife?"

"It's grandfather's."

"My father's knife? How did you end up with it?"

"Long story."

"Totò, slow down. What drugs did you take?"

Charlie puts his hand on my twitching shoulder and tries to calm me down and stop my butchering. He can't.

Simone looks at Charlie and then at me. She appears mildly amused at the panic she has unleashed. Her eyes, more beautiful than ever, are impeccably made-up, with a deep pink eye-shadow exaggeratedly smeared and trailing to the corner, her long seductively batting eyelashes, movie-like, winking at me. Her response to my attack angers me even more.

And as I look into her eyes, the impossible begins to happen.

Very slowly, almost imperceptibly, the arm holding the knife slides in deeper and deeper, going right under the dangling muscles and into the fatty tissues. It is an out-of-control slow motion that, as I bend in half, first draws in my right shoulder and then my head. Soon my left side follows, dragging in my other shoulder, my other arm, my chest, my stomach, and my thighs. My whole shrinking body is slipping into Simone's distended stomach cavity, and then everything goes dark. I feel but can't see; yet I am not surprised that the cut is sucking me in. It is a slow unstoppable ingestion, a motion not so much unpleasant as frighteningly bizarre, and I need to make it stop before it gets worse.

"Charlie, help me."

The sound of my voice, coming from inside of Simone, resonates like a distant, muted echo.

"*Porco diavolo* what did you do?"

His cursing, also muffled, reaches me from far away.

"For fuck sakes Charlie, will you help me or not!"

My body is almost completely inside Simone, when finally, heeding my call for assistance, I feel Charlie's hands on my ankles.

"Get out of there!" he screams.

He momentarily anchors my legs against his body by pulling me towards him, and I stop sliding forward. It doesn't last. Simone, much stronger than the both of us, inhales deeply, and in one powerful heave, swallows the rest of me. Charlie, hands firmly gripped to my ankles, has no choice but to follow me into her.

"Look what you have done. I'm all dirty," Charlie complains.

ଊ

Inside Simone, I stand up and then Charlie stands up, I begin to walk and then Charlie walks. For a while we walk side by side as if going on a hike, not saying much.

"We shouldn't have gone in. Everything is closed, it's not allowed," he says.

I put my arm under his, holding on Italian style, and in the darkness we feel our way forward.

Simone begins to breathe heavily, and my head begins to pound. The vigour of her inhalation slams Charlie and me against the layers of rippled and stacked small intestines; it releases us for a second and then smacks us against the outside of these strange sausage-like casings. The process is repeated at brief intervals and it begins to hurt. I double over under the painful pressure that has my head in a vise-grip. I put my hands to my head, and squeeze to make it stop, but to no use.

"Charlie, are you with me."

"Cousin, what do you suggest?"

"Let's make our way to her other side."

"The other side of who? Of what? And you know Simone is going to kill you; you ruined her dress."

My eyes quickly adjust to the insides of Simone, and, using my grandfather's knife, I turn left and begin carving a corridor for Charlie and me. Fighting our way through her becomes a matter of survival. It is a way to stymie the internal pulling and pushing that is crushing my skull.

We find a small path between the colon and the small intestine which releases some of the pressure, but walking gets increasingly more difficult, the passage narrows, the obstacles get bigger, and the terrain becomes uneven.

This inner darkness is imbued with the redness and wetness of Simone's blood. We make our way tentatively, and I balance myself on a malleable and slippery flooring of pulsating bowels. I bend over to walk through the low passage and use my head against the colon above to sustain myself. Crouching down, Charlie follows me.

He should be happy that I'm carving a passage for the both of us. The tunnel is a dark red, a sanguine hue; colours that one finds in the pulp of a ripe Sicilian orange and not the bright reds of a flesh wound. I try to explain this difference to Charlie.

"Totò, stop waiving that knife, and stop talking nonsense."

"I can't."

"You have to, you're destroying everything."

I'm having problems distinguishing what he is saying from what he means. There is a disarticulation or a displacement of words and thoughts that is beyond my control.

What I know is that I can't afford to stop. I continue walking, turning slightly left, avoiding natural obstacles of overhanging filaments and tendons.

This is not an easy journey. There are uncontrollable urges that are pulling and pushing, my head inflates and deflates, while my lungs feel the crushing weight of her breathing. The ground is wet and slippery, overgrown and moss-like. We trip over jarring bones and sink into pockets of fat. There are forces at play within this cavity that can only be counteracted by aggressively hacking through sinewy innards and dangling muscles. Each puncture by my uncle's knife brings a mist of red that also stains my hands, but I don't care.

I'm practically running in order to quickly get to the other side, but Charlie has difficulties keeping up.

"Cousin, stop for a minute, what are you cutting up, leave them alone, you're going to hurt yourself. Come down, where are you going?"

Hacking back and forth I carve a path through a jungle of body parts whose names I forget. The trail in front and behind is lit by a weak light coming through the entrance. I make a mistake and slice through a main artery of some sort, a casing that empties at our feet. Guck rushes towards us and makes walking more of a muddied, swamp-like affair.

"Salvatore, get out of there, you're making a mess."

I'm annoyed that he doesn't see the big picture and that all he cares about is to not get dirty. He doesn't understand how important it is for both of us to get to the other side.

Charlie, winded, again pleads for me to stop running.

The pressure in my head suddenly abates and I enter a niche between the liver and the kidney in order to rest against Simone's soft gall bladder, and to allow Charlie to catch up.

Charlie, sweating and out of breath, looks at me funny, and then, concerned, wipes off strands of tissue and pieces of ligaments from my hair and my shoulders.

"What a mess you've made. You have to stop this."

"Me? It was her. She wouldn't let me go, she wouldn't believe that I am not gay, that I'm not like you guys."

"Us guys?"

"You know what I mean."

"So you're not gay, but you kiss a man, and you say it like there is something wrong with being gay."

"You're a real idiot, that's not what I'm saying."

"I'm teasing you, silly boy."

Suddenly the heavy breathing of Simone starts again and I stand up and begin climbing. I am pounded against the liver and then against the kidney, and I fall down. Uncaring, I carve us a hole to the right towards the stomach.

"Here, have some," I tell Charlie.

Blood specks cover my face, and I can't avoid tasting those flecks as they land on my lips, but unlike the taste of the blood from a bleeding finger, the taste in my mouth is the tartness of a Sicilian orange, and because of that and not because I like the taste of blood, I lick my lips and enjoy running my tongue over those speckles that evoke a better childhood.

I nick some of the entrails that are reachable and pass them on to Charlie so that he can dispose of them as he wishes.

"By the way, I saw you dancing… I saw the way you kissed Simone."

"What are you talking about?"

He smiles and nods as if he knows something that I don't know.

"It was her, she was all over me. She kissed me first. I'm not gay. I didn't want her."

He continues to smile.

"It's not for me to say, but it looked like you were enjoying yourself, and there is nothing wrong with that."

I don't like his innuendoes. He wants me to think that I am like him. So that he can then say that it's normal to be queer. There is no way that I am like him, look at him, with those heels and that dress.

"Fuck you Charlie… It wasn't like that."

"Okay."

"And besides, I was drunk."

"Okay, whatever you say. But you know, cousin, that being drunk is only an excuse, not a reason. I know about excuses. My clients are full of them."

"You're an idiot, Charlie, I felt nothing."

"Why so defensive, cousin? We're just talking. We can be honest."

He's a fucking idiot and is now getting on my nerves.

He looks at me and smiles, which irritates me even more.

I start throwing things at him. At first they're small pieces, like the chunks of dark liver that I've been holding in my hands. I find bigger ones, heavier ones that have fallen on the ground, and throw them as well.

I miss and he laughs, "There is no shame in being gay, you should try it, oh sorry, you already did…"

He can't stop giggling at what he thinks is funny. The more he laughs, the angrier I get. He has no right. I'm going to fucking hit him.

I pick up with two hands the massive entrails that litter the ground and fling them as hard as I can. He hides, cowardly, between the colon and the large intestine while I continue to bombard him with anything I can find, lift and toss. Still unsteady, I keep missing, which infuriates me. I rush to where he's hiding, and brusquely drag him out into the open.

"Charlie stop laughing or I'll smack you."

He continues to cackle and I make a fist.

"You're one to talk."

I point to his dress, to his shoes, and to the bright red lipstick that he has re-applied.

"Look at yourself. And tell me something. Do you like sucking cocks, dressed as a woman? Because I got to tell you *that's* pretty disgusting. Do you know what *you're* putting in your mouth? And for what, for twenty Euros; it's fucking sickening."

He stops laughing.

"That's mean, cousin, I was just teasing."

My head is throbbing and I can't make it stop. I can't think clearly right now, but I know that I didn't do anything wrong, and that I hate this stupid gender-bending bullshit, that I've had enough of everyone's games, and that they can all go to hell, Charlie included.

"Fuck you Charlie; you got me into this mess by bringing me here, I never wanted to come in the first place."

"It's a lie, cousin, you had a choice, and you certainly don't have the right to insult me. It's unfair to say that. I think people always know what they are doing, even when they lie to themselves. I'm not the enemy here. Do you always blame others?"

Great, now the fucked-up cousin is lecturing me?

"You're finished? You want to do me a favour, then, leave me alone. Better yet, get the fuck out of here. Leave; go back to *La barca* and your queer friends. Pick me up on the way home when you're done being a whore. I'm sick and tired of this whole gay, man-woman shit. I don't belong here, and you know it. And by the way, I can blame who I want to blame."

I've had enough.

I turn my back to him, my meanness surprises even me, but he deserves it.

He walks away to find a new path.

Angrily slashing to the left and to the right, I work frantically, ignoring Charlie and his ridiculous implications and his ridiculous women's clothes, his ridiculous friends, and his ridiculous Sicilian ways.

He's taking my mother's side. Saying that it was my choice means I'm to blame. That's a good one, again blame the victim. Classic.

Going up is a dead end. My head hurts even more now. Simone's densely packed large intestine is a setback; it's blocking the way. I still want to get to the other side.

Ironically, concentrating on the obstacle in front of me calms me down.

He's full of shit. I got excited. Horny even, I admit. For a moment I forgot who I was, where I was, but that's all. I thought Simone was a woman. It was a mistake.

The bowels are thickly stacked and the more I carve into them the more there seems to be. A mistake, like all the other mistakes, but telling my father was not a mistake, I wanted him to know.

*Son, that's all I was saying. I just wanted you to admit that.*

So what. Go away.

After an hour, I have barely made a dent into the rippled barrier of entangled casings that closes in around me.

Still I have to ask Charlie something about this gay thing.

He's not behind me anymore and I almost don't care; prefer it. But I just have to ask one thing and then I'm done with him, with my mother and with everyone else.

But now, he's nowhere to be found. He must be furious. I was mean, but fuck him, he pissed me off. I swear I didn't want Simone; I just got way too drunk for my own good.

I see him. He is behind some cartilage, standing by himself, away from where bile and blood is spewing out of holes I'm punching in.

He looks sad and hurt. I feel sorry. I am sorry.

Okay, he's right, I enjoyed kissing Simone and I did get turned on, and it was exciting, and I felt alive, and it felt good, and it was right, and it wasn't wrong. I admit it, but does it make me gay?

"Charlie, come."

"You sure you want me along. I'm disgusting, remember."

"Yes, come on… you idiot."

"And you'll stop acting like a maniac and stop insulting me."

Charlie follows me to the other side of the intestine and, feeling less anxious, we are back to the crossroads, where the liver meets the kidney.

"Charlie, and don't fuck around, be honest… Does what I did with Simone mean that I could be… Gay, have gay tendencies?"

"Cousin Sal, is that what is bothering you? I was going to tell you, but you were being impossible, and you didn't let me finish. Gays don't usually go for what you call she-males, for people like Simone, for people like me. Our clients are pretty much all straight. That's for sure. But you know straight and gays, it's not about just two types, you know, everyone is a bit different, you understand, we're all here and there, we're just sexual people, you shouldn't think too much, it means less than you think. I can assure you, you're not gay… But if you want to try my dress…."

He laughs, and I appreciate the joke as well as the honesty. He hasn't totally convinced me, but I feel much better.

"Cousin, don't worry about it. It was just a kiss."

"It's not that easy."

"I think you were letting yourself be sensual, sexual, open, you were in a moment, it's not a bad thing."

Was it not more than that? Maybe not.

My lower back hurts. My heads begins to pound again. Charlie doesn't know why we have to keep on moving. I explain our situation to him, and how we got to be where we are.

In Simone's body, it's very natural. Our real proportions are no longer important; the concept of size has disappeared, creating an even playing field where everything is proportionate. We are as large or as small as her liver when my blade touches it and we are proportional to her kidney when my blade cuts into its odd bean shape. Seeing and not seeing becomes the same, we are in total darkness and yet we can see in limited blacks and reds and find our direction by what appears to be ancestral memory. We seem to know where we are meant to go, without really knowing.

He ignores my explanation.

"Cousin Salvatore, my turn to ask you something. You've been strange since dinner, probably something my father said? Is that what got you going?"

"Yes, no. I'm not sure. I have a lot on my mind... One minute some things are clear, the next they're not. Charlie, have you ever thought that something important happened one way, and you are sure about it, but then you learn that it may not have been like that."

"What?"

"Never mind."

"*Per favore*, tell me. It is interesting."

"You know that story that your father told tonight... The one about me running away, well there is more to it, there was a reason for my running away...."

I tell Charlie everything.

He isn't surprised; he pretty well guessed what happened between my mother and his father, before I tell him.

"And that is what has been bothering you? All those years? You know my father. He did things like that, his whole life.

Everyone knows he was a lady's man… Still tries to be. I'm not even sure I'm my mother's son. People think that I'm adopted, or better, the adopted son of one of his mistresses."

The fact that my mother might have been one of many doesn't comfort me. What happened wasn't trivial, it screwed up my life.

"Charlie, it was my mother!"

"And you've been angry at that for thirty years?"

"Shouldn't I have been? What are you saying, Charlie?"

"Excuse me my dear cousin, but you've wasted your time staying angry."

"You're an idiot."

"Now you're going to start again with your insults."

I shouldn't have said anything. People never understand, unless they're in your shoes, and not even then. Yes, I'm angry, it's always there, always has been.

I go back to work. A large piece of the liver is cut and dislodged and now we have more space. I look around the cavity. The blood has stopped running, and where there is blood, it no longer looks like blood, it has become more like wrinkled sheets of shiny burgundy-coloured paper. It is blood that on impact with the knife coagulates into, at first a gel, and then later a palpable material very similar to drying papier-mâché, which then turns into crinkled wrapping paper.

"Cousin, I am sorry, but what my father did, what your mother did, and what your father didn't do, none of that is about you, that's what I mean."

"What are you talking about? Yes it was. It fucked me up, and I resent them all for that. No, I hate them for that, and nobody should deny me that."

I certainly don't need pop psychology from a guy in a dress who didn't finish high school.

My shoes are getting soaked, my feet are getting cold. I step out of the murky pool, and find a passageway made of intertwined muscles and yellowish fat. He follows me there.

"I didn't mean to hurt your feelings. You can't keep hating people, you're only hurting yourself. Look at me."

I walk away from him. I don't want to talk to him. I work myself into a frenzy, carving where I can cut by feel, becoming more tactile, enjoying the different textures against my fingers. I deliberately run my hand against the uneven surface. What does he mean by 'it's wrong to blame them for who I am'. Maybe it's about him, he doesn't want to blame his parents for being gay, but that's different.

I feel the mesh-like tissues and the sponge-like cells before cutting through; it is when I stumble into an entanglement of thick muscles that cutting becomes almost impossible. I dig down, and I excavate. I stumble, fall and bounce back, redoubling my efforts. I imagine hacking through my anger, slicing through my uncle, and then through my mother. It is not about Simone anymore, it's about everyone. I sink my hands into the gunk, letting it slither between my fingers, enjoying the sensation.

I have to reluctantly admit that I always knew that my uncle did not force my mother. Charlie could be right. And what if I had not told my father? Everything might have been different.

I'm so busy thinking and forging ahead that I forget about Charlie, and when I do remember and turn around, he is no longer there. Where did he go?

It was easy to blame; I had ready-made excuses, which I have relied on whenever I've failed. He actually makes sense.

Finding my way back to the large intestine, I hold on to dangling filaments and go look for him. I find an old route and follow it to where we had been.

Why can't I admit that I told my father so that he would no longer go away and stay with me?

Because it backfired.

So now I'm confused. Who am I angry at, who should I have really been blaming? Myself? Is Charlie right? Where is he?

I begin to worry that I might have lost him, that he might have fallen, that *he* might have left me.

"CHARLIE!"

I keep screaming, but all I hear is the gurgling of Simone's stomach.

"CHARLIE! Where are you?"

I run madly towards the entrance to the wound, to where we had come in, and there, backlit by the outside light, a shadow in a dress and high heels is sitting on a stump.

He wasn't hurt, he wasn't scared, he wasn't lost, he wasn't looking for me; he was simply gazing into space.

"Charlie, what happened to you?"

He looks at me as if addressing a young child and says, "Totò, I'm tired of your craziness... You've got to stop running. It's almost morning. You may get hurt. It's a mess...."

"Charlie, I've been doing a lot of thinking...."

"That's good. Just stop now. Sit down. Rest. Put the knife away."

It seems important to him that I listen, and if it makes him happy I will.

"Okay."

I look at the knife and uncle was right, it is a beautiful blade, which reminds me that I also blamed being born Sicilian for way too long, and that should also stop. I caress the bone handle. Charlie is preoccupied; he hesitates and searches for the right words. Waiting for him to compose himself, I find a smooth surface behind where we are sitting and carve into Simone, 'Salvatore and Charlie were here'.

He becomes serious. "Very nice, Salvatore, now put the knife away."

"What's wrong Charlie?"

He stares ahead, and then behind him.

"We should go home cousin."

"I know I've been a bit of an asshole. You're upset, is it me?"

"No, it's not that, but you're not the only one with problems, Salvatore."

"You mean you, and the transvestite thing, the being gay thing?"

I was going to add, the being a prostitute thing, but suddenly I feel sorry for him.

"Actually my parents still don't know, well my father maybe suspects it, but he won't say, too much shame and the rest of the town fears him so they won't say anything to his face. But, they know and I play the game by pretending that they don't know. You know, like Pirandello says, we Sicilians like to pretend… but it's not that. Salvatore, the truth is, why do I bother with all this, with staying in Sicily, with the dishonesty? What's here for me? Can you tell me?"

Having no advice for Charlie, I just listen.

"I want to leave, I'm a coward for staying…."

"I don't want to pretend anymore…."

"If I don't do something I swear I'm going to die. I'm going crazy here. I put the face on but some days I just want to lay down and die. I'm trapped…."

His words make me realize how I had also trapped myself, and how it had started the day I told my father. I had been caught in an anger trap of my own creation. It wasn't them, it was me. Being sober sucks.

"I would go to Tunis."

"I have a friend in Tunis. Remember I told you."

Poor Charlie, at this moment, he looks so fragile. He brings his knees together and pats down his party dress that is blotched with dirt. Looks at his red shoes with the thin straps.

"They're ruined…."

"You know Sal, I want to escape this town, this island…."

"His name his Farouk…."

The same name as the singer, and I ask about the connection. He looks at me, smiles, and then I understand who this Farouk is; it is one and the same.

"He loves me for who I am…."

Two men in love still sounds strange, even gross, but not as disgusting as I might have thought earlier.

Again that smile, and I recognize the look of someone who believes he is in love, one who is at the beginning of love, when love is all about feelings, about passion, about desire. But then, he's talking about another man, someone named *Farouk.* Charlie is in love with a gay Tunisian singer. Poor Charlie. I thought I had problems.

"Farouk says that I can work at the bar where he plays regularly in Tunis. I mean I'd do dishes or be a waiter. I'd pay my way. I don't care; I just want to be with him. I'm ready to go, but I'm afraid."

All that's missing is for Charlie to say that Farouk is his soulmate, and I'll barf, but I can't be mean anymore. I realise he truly is in love, whatever that means. It's in the face. I had that look when I first met Susan. Speaking of Susan, what am I going to tell her? I guess I have to tell her everything, if I want to start clean. I notice Charlie's tattoo and I worry about him. I point to it, and tell him I hope he's not thinking of doing something stupid.

"No cousin, I am not ready for that. Farouk says that this tattoo was the first thing he noticed about me and it made him so sad that he had to come over and talk to me. It used to represent desperation but now it means hope."

"He came to *La barca*. That night we danced so much, we talked and we got along really good. He's really nice," he giggles. "He's also so gorgeous… We speak almost every day. He doesn't understand why I don't leave, but it's not easy. He gets mad at me, but you understand, right? It's impossible…."

This relationship seems so important to Charlie, but he's right, it's impossible. But really, a long-distance relationship, the gay thing, the Tunisian thing, the culture thing, could Charlie be creating any more problems for himself? My gut reaction is to say no, that he is going to make things worse.

"I've been saving some of my money. I have enough to get me started down there. I am putting aside all I can. My cell phone is my only expense. Well, and the clothes, and the shoes…."

At the word clothes, Charlie gives me the same look Susan has when she comes home after having been at the mall a bit too long and spent a bit too much on the purchase of a new dress or fancy shoes. He's such a girl, and I don't mean it as a bad thing anymore.

"If it doesn't work out, I will try Rome or somewhere else." He laughs, "Maybe Canada, because once I go, I go."

"Charlie, I really need a drink."

"This is all I have."

He lights a joint and passes it to me. It's been a while since I've inhaled. I choke, two or three small coughs, and he laughs at me. I laugh back. The smoke makes me light-headed.

So now am I supposed to forgive everyone, let them get away with what they did?

The internal workings of Simone had given us a moment of respite, but they are now at work again. Each time she takes a breath we are pushed further in, released as she exhales, only to be sucked in again with the next breath. I try to synchronize my breathing with hers but it doesn't work. In these circumstances it is difficult to know what to do. The pressure to move forward, to carve some more, comes back as strong as ever. Anxiety arrives and leaves in waves.

If everyone is to blame, no one is to blame? Where does it leave me? There is something fucked-up about this.

"Totò, what do you think I should do?"

I don't know what to say. I'm not the advice-giving type.

"Forget it. You know if I leave, I can never come back to Petra. It's not easy. You can't just get up and go. I know I want to, but my father will butcher me and my mother will surely die of a broken heart…."

I think about how much I have held back from everyone, how I've refused to show myself, how afraid I've been to take action and how I'm getting worse, at how much time I have wasted being angry, making myself unhappy. How righteous I have made my unhappiness. Okay, fine, but where is the fucking resolution?

"Come Charlie, let's walk some more."

We move forward and find an old path and follow it to where the trail ends and opens into what looks like a playground. Everything is so serious.

"Charlie, let's have fun."

Simone's breathing gets faster and faster and we are shaken. I'm thrown against her taut skin that acts as a fence. Luckily it is between two ribs and it hurts less, between the two posts. It feels like I am bouncing off a vertical trampoline. By pressing against the membrane and fatty tissues that are behind the muscles, I can touch the skin of Simone's back and I know that we are very close to the other side. I have carved all the way through.

"I'm scared, Salvatore, I have always been scared. I can dress as a woman, dance in drag, go down on a complete stranger... But leaving Petra, leaving Sicily... It scares me, I'm so afraid...."

"I don't want to be a whore all my life. I want something better...."

"You know Salvatore, Farouk says that we're not kids anymore, that we *can* think on our own, he says that we make our own destiny. That may be a cliché but he's right, and he really wants me to join him...."

He takes out another joint and lights it. Sucks in as deeply as he can, like he did earlier, holds it for longer than he should and lets it out. He passes the smoke to me, and I shouldn't after all I have ingested tonight, but that thought only lasts long enough for me to grab the joint and inhale as deeply and as long as Charlie. This time I don't cough. Maybe it will finally make the pounding in my head go away.

"Farouk also said that I shouldn't be so hard on my parents and my situation because I am the product of what has happened to me and what I have made of it and that he loves me for who I have become. I think it's the same for you. Farouk is sweet. I love him so much...."

I'm not sure it's that simple, but that is what people in love would say and he is in love. I still can't wrap my head around his kind of love. We take turns passing the joint, not talking, just thinking and staring ahead. I don't feel as angry anymore. I look at him.

Maybe there is no resolution.

"Cousin Charlie, you're a great guy, Farouk is a lucky man to have found you, you're a good person, and I must tell you without a lie, you make one hell of a good looking woman. The prettiest I have seen tonight. Whatever you do you will always be the prettiest."

"Thank you, cousin Sal, that's the nicest thing you've said to me all night."

He smiles and kisses me on the cheek.

"Maybe it's just the dope talking. Kidding. Speaking of which, Charlie, what do I tell Susan?"

"Do you love her?"

"More than ever, and I'm actually glad she dragged me back to Sicily. I feel better than I have in long time."

"Well Cousin, Farouk says that in Tunisia they have a saying that a person is allowed to take one secret to the grave. You can decide if this is it."

I play with the knife, twirl it, open and close it and then I get an idea.

I get up, feel for a weakness in the canvas, and make a slight piercing. From the inside, I cut a small hole into Simone's back. The skin easily gives and I slice to the left of two vertebrae. I rip apart an opening for us.

"Charlie, come and see...."

Before I can finish my sentence, there is a whoosh, a sea wind, and suddenly with the breach, the colours become brighter, my breathing normalizes, and the pounding in my head slows down. Morning light peers through the opening, and I feel great.

I quickly enlarge the perforation, creating a sort of window. Soon my whole hand is outside. The greater the gap, the better I feel, and the brighter it gets in here. Charlie comes beside me and we both look outside. The hole is now big enough to let our heads through, and what we see is breathtaking.

I put the knife away.

Outside of Simone there is a beautiful African desert of soft undulating two-dimensional sand dunes. A large red sun is in the horizon with one solitary palm tree encased in a cement planter nearer to the sidewalk.

It is not like peering outside of a tall thin black man dressed as a woman who calls herself *La Marocchina*. It is as if we are simply looking out of a window, out of a freighter's porthole that has transported us to Africa where the morning sun is a plastic red disc. We have journeyed further than imaginable. We are no longer outside of *La barca*, or outside of Trapani or even in Sicily, but in a new continent, near the edge of a desert. We have dug a tunnel under the Mediterranean Sea and come out in Africa.

Nearby there are road signs, with oversized blue arrows pointing in different directions. To our left is Tunis, to our right is Sousse, and in front of us is Algeria, and as far as the eye can see there is an ocean of sand.

"Totò, is this where you wanted to go?"

His face is incredulous, but not totally surprised.

"Look," I say.

Below us, farther away, veiled by the sun's morning rays, a man is coming towards us. It is the hazy silhouette of a Berber.

I recognize this wiry man with the blue turban. The dirty-white jellaba, and the angular face with a sparse and scraggly goatee are very familiar.

He is pulling a camel along. He sees us looking at him and is shocked to see us up there. Together, man and beast make their way closer. The Berber stops right underneath us, looks up, and blinks under the bright morning sun.

“يقيرفال ةيطم ديرت له,” he says in Arabic, or in a Sicilian that we don't quite understand.

He repeats what may be a greeting or an order. “طقست. وروال ةرشعب.”

“What's he saying?”

The Berber, who keeps talking to us in his own language, impervious to the fact that we don't understand him, shouts, “يقيرفال ةيطم ديرت له.”

He motions for us to come down, to jump on his one-hump camel. To make that leap easier, he positions his animal just below our newly-created opening, below the elevated ridge of the Botanical Gardens, below the grove of blood orange trees that peek over the fence.

The Berber smiles, motions with a quick downward wave, and throws at us a slew of more Arabic that we still don't get. He also wants ten Euros, and that we understand.

“Totò, what should we do?”

“Charlie, it's our chance to get a ride to Tunis.”

“You think?”

“Yes. Charlie, you go first.”

“I'm afraid.”

“I'm here. I won't let you fall.”

I stand to the side and wait. Suddenly full of courage, Charlie makes a decision, turns himself around, pulls his dress up, steps over the makeshift aperture and lowers his body.

Halfway down, he stops.

"I can't go on, Salvatore. I can't do it. I'm afraid of camels."

I feel sorry for him; he was so close. I should do something.

Charlie gives up, lifts himself up using his arms and by holding on to the edge. He hauls one leg over and tries to set his knee on the ridge of the wall in order to climb back up inside the Gardens.

"Help me cousin."

I don't know if I understood him to say help me, in the sense of saying help me make a decision as opposed to saying help me climb back in, but suddenly, and quite lucidly, I am certain that he truly means for me to help him decide and I decide to truly help him.

With my hands, I push his knee right off the ledge.

"Salvatore?"

"Come on Charlie, you can do it."

Charlie is now back outside of where we were, hanging onto the ledge, his body fully stretched out under this portal, his high heels almost touching the saddle of the short Arabian camel.

The smiling Berber encourages him, "وروال ةرشعب .طقست."

I grab one of Charlie's hands and then the other, but instead of pulling him up like he wants me to, I gently bend and lower him until his shoes touch the sun-dried saddle of a very patient dromedary, and then when his feet are secure on the camel, I open one hand. Charlie holds on to my fingers a bit longer and then I let go. Having no choice, he crouches and I let go of his other hand as he settles on the saddle.

I poke my head and shoulders out to better look at him, and there on the desert sand, the Berber, on foot, and holding on to the camel's reins, guides this makeshift sand taxi towards Tunis. Charlie turns around, nervous, smiling, and waves at me.

I smile and wave back.

The Arab asks me to wait. He says, in Sicilian, that he can only take one person at a time, that I will have to wait my turn, and that I shouldn't worry; that God willing he'll be back.

Québec, Canada
2009